TOO LATE
FOR REGRETS
Liza Hadley

Harlequin Books

TORONTO • NEW YORK • LONDON
AMSTERDAM • PARIS • SYDNEY • HAMBURG
STOCKHOLM • ATHENS • TOKYO • MILAN
MADRID • WARSAW • BUDAPEST • AUCKLAND

Special thanks and acknowledgment to Liza Hadley

ISBN 0-373-15300-7

TOO LATE FOR REGRETS

Unpublished Edition Copyright © 1993 by Liza Hadley.

This edition Copyright © 1995 by Harlequin Enterprises B.V.

One

A tremor ran the full length of Cathy's spine as she stepped into the hotel's ornately styled, gilt lift, so typically Italian in design and so like the one which she remembered from Castel di Bellano.

"Don't worry, my dear. It may look old-fashioned but I'm sure it's quite safe."

Cathy blinked in surprise, suddenly realizing that the reassuring observation must have been directed at her.

The other woman smiled kindly. "You've gone quite pale. Perhaps you would have been better using the stairs."

Or perhaps I'd have been better not returning to Italy at all, Cathy thought dispiritedly. It wasn't the possible unreliability of the lift which worried her; it was being here, back in Florence, the very city where Nic lived and worked, with all its unhappy memories, which was setting her nerves on edge.

Had it been a mistake offering to take Diane's place on this assignment? She'd thought that after five years she was up to returning but perhaps she'd misjudged the power of her memory. It didn't feel like five years since she'd last been here, it felt like yesterday. But if it had been a mistake, it was too late for regrets now.

She swallowed. "No...really...I'm alright...thank you. Look, we're here now...safely on the ground floor." She stood aside, allowing the older woman to precede her into the corridor.

"Are you attending the cookery course too?" the woman enquired as they headed in the same direction down the passage.

"In a way. I'm reviewing it for the magazine I work for...*Cuisine for Cooks,*" Cathy explained, glad to get her thoughts focusing on the present rather than the past.

"Really? How exciting. I buy the magazine every month. You're a journalist then?"

"A feature writer."

"And you're here to write about this new holiday course."

Cathy nodded. "Mmm... It's something different, and we think a lot of our readers will be interested in it."

"I'm sure they will. I love Italian food but what really attracted me was the fact that there are sightseeing excursions as well as the cookery workshops. Italy's such a lovely country, don't you think?"

There was a moment's silence while Cathy struggled to find her voice. "Yes...it is."

How hard that admission was to make. Five years ago Nic had soured everything associated with Italy for her. At nineteen, she'd been a naive, impressionable teenager, still hurt by the breakup of her parents' marriage and very vulnerable. Nic had seemed like the man of her dreams...the man of every woman's dreams until... Cathy shook her head and cut the painful thought short before it could reach fruition.

She caught a glimpse of her reflection in a mirror as they passed, and unconsciously her chin tilted. In her loosely styled linen suit, her chestnut gold hair coiled in a stylish chignon, she looked a capable, mature woman.

She was twenty-four now and wiser. She wasn't going to allow a disastrous, teenage *fling* to get the better of her like this.

"Mmm, have you seen the food?" the woman enquired as they entered the large dining room.

Special effort had been made for the inaugural reception evening and a table stretched the length of one wall, groaning with the weight and variety of food dishes set out on it. There were numerous pasta dishes in creamy meat and vegetable sauces: *carbonara, gnocchi, caponata, tortelli, pansoti, linguine,* and for dessert: *bocconotti, cassata, zabaglione, tiramisu, ricciarelli.* Cathy's professional mind ran easily through the list as she took a deep breath and forced her stomach muscles to relax.

She was going to enjoy the week ahead and nothing, certainly not thoughts of Nicolas Lucciano, was going to spoil it for her.

"Excuse me, dear. I must just go and have a word with the couple over there. I met them on the plane coming over. I'll see you later." The woman excused herself.

Left alone, Cathy took one of the glasses of chilled white wine from the silver tray proffered by a waiter.

"Ah! Miss Walker... How are you settling in? I trust your room is to your liking. It is one of the hotel's best, I believe."

Cathy returned Giulio Savatini's welcoming smile. He was the course organiser and coordinator. His rotund build made him a perfect recommendation for his country's cuisine. "It's lovely. I'm delighted with it," she assured him.

"The hotel has recently been refurbished. It had been rundown for some time until a local businessman bought it last

year. He has spent a lot of money on improvements," Giulio
informed her solemnly.

"It's in a good location. I'm sure it will prove a good investment," Cathy said politely.

"I expect it will," Giulio agreed. "The first cooking
demonstration will commence promptly at nine-thirty
tomorrow morning," he said, changing the subject. "An
hour's break for lunch, then sightseeing in the afternoons.
Will you be joining us on our outings? We plan to spend at
least two afternoons in Florence itself," Giulio told her
persuasively.

A slight tremor shook Cathy as Giulio's words brought
back memories of a day spent in the city with Nic, visiting
the Cathedral and the Uffizi, one of the world's most
famous art galleries, and then laughingly passing down the
narrow space between that and the Piazza della Signoria
where long arcades housed numerous stalls piled high with
the usual tourist souvenirs. She'd tried on a huge straw hat
which Nic had promptly bought her, declaring it the best
example of haute couture he'd ever seen.

"I don't think so. I've visited Florence before. A l-long
time ago," Cathy told him, appalled to hear the slight
wobble in her voice.

She was furious with herself for this display of weakness.
How many women would still allow themselves to get so
upset over a man who'd callously rejected them five years
before? She blinked furiously, forcing the imminent threat
of tears into retreat. This was ridiculous. Why did she have
to keep thinking of Nic? Besides, he must be what...thirty-
two or thirty-three now? He was probably married! Her
stomach muscles cramped. Why was that thought so ridiculously painful?

Several more people had arrived and the room seemed full of small, chattering groups. With a huge effort of will, Cathy forced herself to smile as her gaze passed from one to another. Suddenly she froze and her heart seemed literally to stop beating.

Then his eyes met hers and she knew that it really was him. Nic was here, only feet away from her. The room seemed to spin.

"Ah! I see Signor Lucciano has arrived. Let me introduce you." The hand on her elbow was Giulio's, leading her, like a lamb to the slaughter, to the very spot where Nic stood.

"Miss Walker, may I introduce Signor Lucciano?"

Cathy's stunned gaze rose to the tall, broad-shouldered man standing in front of her.

"Introductions are not necessary, Giulio. Miss Walker and I already know each other," Nic said starkly. Only the barest civility threaded his tones and his eyes were like chips of black ice as they stared down at her.

Momentarily struck dumb, Cathy could only stare helplessly back at him. She realized, with mounting dismay, that Nic was as devastatingly attractive as ever. His Italian ancestry had produced the kind of dark, brooding good looks that women adored. His jet black hair was thick and sleek, his eyes dark to the point of blackness, his features finely chiselled, his hard mouth ruthless yet sensual.

At last Cathy managed to summon some remnant of an intellect almost completely shattered by his appearance.

"Nic... This is a...a surprise." Surprise! She felt chilled to the bone with shock. "It's been a long time. It must be..."

"Five years," he supplied coldly.

She swallowed, "I-Is it really that long?"

"You had forgotten?"

Her palms grew damp with perspiration. It was four years, ten months and twenty-six days since they'd last met. "No... I hadn't forgotten," she admitted, forcing a stilted smile to her lips.

There was no responding smile in Nic's expression as his ruthless gaze held hers. "How could you? I understand that however unsavoury the circumstances, no woman forgets her first—

"Trip abroad?" Cathy interrupted in a rush, a fiery ball of scarlet replacing the previous pallor of her skin. Nic hadn't been about to say what she thought he'd been about to say, had he? Not in front of Giulio Savatini? Her green eyes widened in mute appeal.

"Quite so," Nic agreed at last, though not one shred of sympathy for her dismay softened the harsh angles of his face. "It *was* your first holiday abroad as I recall."

Relief at the reprieve was tinged with anger. How dare Nic threaten to bring up that painfully humiliating memory? "Holiday is hardly the right word, is it? I was working for my stepfather most of the time," she said tightly.

His dark eyes glittered alarmingly. "You sell yourself short. Wouldn't it be more honest to say that you were working on your stepfather's behalf twenty-four hours a day?"

Cathy frowned uncomprehendingly. Why was his look and his tone so full of disgust? "I—I worked as hard as I could for Harry," she said uncertainly.

"Didn't you just?" Nic jeered under his breath.

Cathy caught the whispered condemnation and felt the nails of her hand bite painfully into her soft palm.

Giulio Savatini's glance went from one to the other of them. "I had no idea that you knew Signor Lucciano," he commented with determined cheerfulness.

Cathy tried to gather up the remnants of her tattered composure. "I—I had no reason to think that Ni—Signor Lucciano would be here."

A cold smile slashed the corners of Nic's mouth. "You are a guest in *my* hotel."

A second shock wave hit Cathy. Nic owned the hotel. What cruel fate had engineered this devastating set of co-incidences? "But your other hotels are all modern... purpose built. They're not like this."

"No," he agreed. "How clever of you to remember."

His look was so chilling that Cathy felt as if she had just been coated in ice.

"Hardly clever. I went to visit several of them, if you re-call," she said stiffly.

"Oh, I do," Nic agreed with disarming swiftness. "But then, you had so many other *duties* to perform as well."

Why did he keep looking at her like that? As if he wanted to murder her. If anyone had a right to such looks it was her, not him. Cathy frowned. "I thought I recognised the lift. It's from Castel di Bellano, isn't it?"

One dark brow arched cynically. "What triggered that particular recollection, I wonder? Its unusual design...or its associations?"

Colour rampaged yet again through Cathy's cheeks. Nic had kissed her once in that lift. Kissed her? What a glori-ous understatement. He had somehow managed to ravage her whole body without his hands ever leaving her shoulders or his lips ever leaving her mouth. Her fingers ached to slap the cruelly insolent look from his face.

Nic's eyes swept over her then returned to her face. "So? What brings you to Florence again? Are you enrolled on this cookery course?"

"No, I'm reviewing it for *Cuisine for Cooks*. One of the other feature writers broke her leg and I stepped in at the last minute." She was babbling nervously, trying to ease the tide of rising panic inside her.

"How very obliging of you. But then, you always were a conscientious worker, weren't you?" Nic stated with dry cynicism, somehow managing to make conscientious sound like a dirty word. "You no longer work for your stepfather then?" Cathy frowned. "I never did work for Harry. The secretarial work I did was only a temporary arrangement." As Nic knew perfectly well.

A cold smile slashed his mouth. "That wasn't quite what I meant. I was referring to Harry's less conventional work practices."

Then, when Cathy continued to stare at him uncomprehendingly, he turned away. "Excuse me. I've just seen someone I must talk to." And with that bald dismissal, he was gone.

Cathy stared after him in mortified silence. Her throat was working in convulsive movements. If she didn't get out of here right now, she was going to do something really embarrassing, like break down and cry. She turned to Mr. Savatini.

"Mr. Savatini, would you excuse me? I think I have a migraine coming on...with the journey and everything...and I really feel it would be better if I got an early night."

"A migraine?" Giulio repeated enquiringly.

Cathy searched hurriedly for the Italian. *"Ho mal di testa?"*

"Ah, a headache," Giulio pronounced sympathetically.

Nausea churned in Cathy's stomach. "I really think an early night is the only answer." And without waiting for a reply, she turned round, brushing unseeing past the clusters of people.

In her room, Cathy tossed her bag down on the bed and went to stand on the balcony overlooking the garden square at the rear of the hotel. Her mind was spinning wildly. After all this time, all these years, she had met Nic again. And what had she done? She hadn't ranted and raved at him, she hadn't hit him, kicked him, she hadn't even coolly ignored him. She felt cheated. Cheated of her chance to vent all the anger and pain and humiliation she'd carried inside her for nearly five years.

Honeysuckle clambered up a trellis on the wall beside the balcony and a profusion of delicate, white flowers spilled their evocative perfume into the air. Honeysuckle had clambered outside her bedroom at Castel di Bellano, too.

Long suppressed images filtered through the defences she had erected. Castel di Bellano...Nic's home...the place where they'd first met.

When Naomi, her mother, had first suggested she should accompany Harry on that business trip to Italy, she hadn't wanted to go. Negotiations were almost complete for a joint venture involving the building of a chain of resort hotels on Italy's Tyrrhenian coast. Two days before he was due to leave, Harry's secretary fell ill and he was left without anyone to accompany him in the role of personal assistant.

Cathy didn't get on particularly well with her stepfather and the thought of spending two weeks in his company was not appealing. Besides, although she'd done a course in office skills at school, her shorthand was nonexistent and her typing painfully slow.

"Can't he just get a temp to go with him?' she'd suggested hopefully.

Naomi had sniffed and looked a little uncomfortable. "Darling, I didn't want to have to tell you this but Harry's business hasn't been doing too well lately. That's why he's so keen to secure the contract with this Lucciano man. Hiring a temporary secretary to go overseas is an expensive undertaking and an outlay he can ill afford at the moment." Naomi's delicate hands fluttered expressively. "After everything that Harry's done for us, how can you not do this one little favour for him?" Naomi had sobbed. "God knows, we'd have been penniless and probably homeless too if it hadn't been for him."

That was a slight exaggeration, Cathy knew. They might not have been exactly wealthy but her father's will had left ample provision for them. Ample for most purposes that was. It wouldn't have stretched to several weeks at health farms during the year or the sets of designer clothes Naomi insisted on buying at the beginning of every season.

Immediately Cathy had regretted that unkind thought and been filled with remorse for not being more understanding.

When her father had walked out on them both four years previously, Naomi had cried on Cathy's shoulder and asked her over and over again why her husband had gone off with another woman... and not even one who was younger and prettier than herself. That Naomi could have understood. But for him to leave her for a woman of the same age who didn't look half as good, was quite beyond her powers of comprehension. And Cathy's too.

When, six months after the divorce, Naomi had married Harry, Cathy had struggled to hide her dismay. He was a bluff, self-important man, so much the opposite of her sensitive intelligent father, that Cathy couldn't imagine what had attracted her mother to him. She'd never liked him but she had tried to accept him for Naomi's sake. After all that her mother had gone through, she felt she owed her that at least.

Just as Cathy had felt she owed it to her mother to go with Harry to Italy.

Thus Cathy had found herself included in the invitation from Nic for her and Harry to stay at his family home, Castel di Bellano, on the outskirts of Florence. Cathy still considered the castle one of the most beautiful homes she'd ever seen with its profusion of towers, spires and minarets.

Their host hadn't been there to meet them. A last minute problem at one of his building sites meant he had been delayed, but his absence hadn't worried Cathy. He was a business associate of Harry's, that was all. If she thought about him at all, it was to picture him as similar in age and appearance to her stepfather: a middle-aged, slightly overweight businessman with glasses and a paunch.

The honeysuckle was powerfully evocative and its perfume played on her senses, rekindling vivid memories of that nineteen-year-old girl leaning out of her bedroom window on her first night in Italy, inhaling the scent of the flowers which twined alongside it.

She'd already changed for dinner, into a sophisticated black dress bought for her by her mother, which showed off her tall, slender figure. A single tear-drop pendant, her only jewellery, nestled in the valley between her breasts.

She hurried out of her bedroom and along the corridor to knock on Harry's bedroom door.

"It's nearly eight o'clock," she reminded him as the door opened.

"I'll be a few minutes yet. Go on down and keep Nic company till I get there." Then Harry winked in a way Cathy didn't much like. "He won't bite, you know."

Thus, reluctantly, she made her way down the broadly curved stairway, wondering which of the huge oak studded doors in the vast entrance hall she should start with. Tentatively she opened the first one she came to.

Rows of portraits graced the walls of the huge room. So absorbed was she in gazing at them that at first she didn't see the man standing beside the enormous stone fireplace. When she did, she jumped.

"Who are you?" she blurted out.

One very dark brow rose at the abruptly delivered question. "I am Nic Lucciano. And you?"

It couldn't be! Cathy's gaze ran over the stranger in a gesture of denial. Where was the paunch, the florid complexion, the flabby physique? This man was tall, well over six feet, and there wasn't an ounce of spare flesh anywhere on his lean frame, superbly emphasised by a black evening suit. Nor could he have been more than about twenty-six or twenty-seven. Even at five feet seven inches, Cathy had to lift her gaze higher and higher to take in the full magnificent whole of him.

"You're Nic Lucciano?" She could only throw back his self-introduction with a disbelieving frown.

"And you, I presume, are Harry's stepdaughter?" Silky, mellifluous tones issued the question, revealing faint amusement and traces of an underlying Italian accent.

"Yes ... I'm Catherine Walker ... but everyone calls me Cathy ... you can too if you like," she suggested, still somewhat dazed by her discovery.

"Cathy ... mmm ... I like that. It suits you," he mused softly.

She felt his dark eyes glide over her, as seductive and as penetrating as a sunbeam, lingering briefly on the delicate swell of her breasts.

Unconsciously, Cathy's fingers flew nervously to the pearl drop pendant at her throat. With difficulty her eyes met his, saw flames dancing in their silky depths and thought for one brief moment of insanity that they were reflecting the flickering conflagration inside her.

"Can I get you a drink?" Nic offered.

"Thank you." Cathy was shocked by the huskiness in her voice.

Nic moved to a discreet drinks cupboard in the corner of the room and poured two glasses of white wine.

"Here, try this," he said, extending a glass to her. "This is produced at the Lucciano vineyards."

"I like it," Cathy pronounced after taking a sip. It was true, but she knew she would have said the same if the wine had tasted like vinegar.

"Are all these portraits of members of your family?" Cathy asked, indicating the rows of huge oil paintings decorating the walls.

"Several generations," Nic said, leading her to the first. "This was the black sheep of the family."

"He looks just like you... or rather, you look just like him."

"I'm not sure that's a compliment." Nic laughed and moved to the next painting. "This was my great-grandmother. She was English, like you. She came to Italy to study art, met my great-grandfather in the Cathedral in Florence and that was it. Love at first sight."

"How romantic. Were they happy together?" Cathy didn't think she could bear it if they hadn't been.

"I believe so. They produced five children so I think they must have been. My grandfather was their eldest son. Now tell me about your family."

A look of pain crossed Cathy's face. "There's really only my mother... and Harry of course. M-my father died in a car accident two years ago."

Unexpectedly Nic's fingers came up to cup her chin and his thumb softly traced the trembling curve of her lip. "I'm sorry," he murmured gently.

Cathy was unprepared for the tremors his touch sent racing through her and she stared up at him, eyes widening in shocked surprise. No man had ever had this effect on her before. Nervously she swung away from him to conceal the heated flush which swept through her.

"And where will your portrait go?" she enquired, trying to sound calm.

Nic pointed to the far end of the wall. "Over there eventually."

"There's an awful lot of space."

"I'm planning to have lots of children to fill it."

"Does your future wife know that?" Cathy enquired, deliberately fishing for information yet unable to stop herself.

Nic slid her an amused look. "Since I haven't met her yet, I doubt it. She'd have to be clairvoyant if she did."

Cathy's heart jumped and warmth flamed her cheeks.

"I guess, though, I can't leave it too much longer if I'm going to compete with my grandfather's record."

In the flickering firelight, his face was all darkness and shadows, his eyes glittering mirrors for the flames, his hard mouth parted slightly in a smile, and in that moment Cathy knew she was lost. In the space of minutes, she had fallen deeply, crazily, in love with Nicolas Lucciano.

* * *

The knock on her door startled Cathy out of her reverie and made her jerk her head upright. Ominously the moon had disappeared behind a cloud and the sky now seemed very, very black. "Who is it?" she demanded.

Even as she spoke, the door was opening. Soft lamplight cast shadows on the wall, making Nic's tall, lean presence unnaturally formidable. Cathy's heart beat wildly in her breast. She left the balcony to come back into the room, diving past Nic to grasp the handle he had just released. The fleeting contact with his body was sufficient to send a shocked charge of electricity racing through her.

Oh God! Surely she couldn't still feel sexually responsive to him? Not after everything that had happened. That would be her body's ultimate betrayal.

"Please . . . go."

Nic's mouth twisted in a humourless smile. "Relax. I have no designs on your body. I only want to talk to you . . . and to bring you these." He drew a small bottle of tablets from his suit pocket. "Painkillers. For your migraine. You do have a migraine, don't you? Giulio Santini asked the manageress if she had anything you could take. He was most concerned."

The faint mockery behind the words made it clear that Guilio's concern was not shared by Nic.

"That was thoughtful of him," Cathy conceded shakily. "But why did you have to bring them?"

"I want to talk to you," Nic informed her coolly. "I have no intention of leaving this room until I've had some answers from you. You owe me that at least."

Owed him? How dare he? Her chin tilted defiantly. "As far as I'm concerned, I don't owe you anything," Cathy retorted, her surge of anger gaining momentum. "How dare you try to embarrass me earlier...in front of Guilio?"

Nic's eyes narrowed to two black, angry slits. "Believe me, if I had been *trying* to embarrass you, I would have succeeded. Consider yourself fortunate."

"Fortunate? To be at the receiving end of your rudeness?" Cathy snapped.

"Fortunate to be at the receiving end of my restraint."

Abruptly silenced by the faint threat inherent in the words, Cathy's tongue ran nervously over her lips. "This is ridiculous," she spluttered at last. "I have no intention of standing here and taking your insults or talking to you."

A jet black brow shot upwards. "That's hardly friendly," he drawled sardonically.

Her fingers clenched tightly on the door handle until her knuckles showed white beneath the skin. "But we can't claim to be friends, can we?"

He said silkily, "Perhaps you would prefer me to use the word *lovers?*"

A flood of scarlet rushed hotly to her cheeks. "Don't say that word!"

"Why? Isn't that what we were?"

Perspiration dampened Cathy's skin and a wave of hysteria threatened to overwhelm her.

"No!" She issued the terse denial through clenched teeth and leaned against the door, desperately in need of its support just to keep herself upright.

To her dismay, Nic began to move towards her. "We *were* lovers," he insisted roughly.

"Once," she conceded painfully. "That's all."

A heartless smile slashed Nic's mouth. "But it was your first time, *cara*. Shouldn't that make it memorable, if nothing else?"

Cathy would never have believed he was capable of such cruelty. This wasn't the same man she had fallen in love with five years ago. What had happened to make him so bitter and cynical? She stared at him, her eyes full of pain, not understanding why he was being so brutal. "I only wish I could forget it ever happened."

"But you can't forget it, can you?"

Green eyes clashed disturbingly with dark ones. She shook her head. "No," she admitted shakily. "I can't."

A look of grim satisfaction darkened Nic's face as his mouth moved closer and closer to hers.

His kiss was like nothing she had ever known before, exploding violently on senses which had scarcely experienced a man's touch in five years. Every shred of reason seemed to desert her as her mouth softened helplessly beneath his, gulping in the strong masculine essence of him like someone falling on fresh water in a desert. The blood raced through her veins, carrying the explosive reverberations to every part of her body until her legs threatened to buckle beneath her.

Just as suddenly as it had begun, the kiss ended. Nic released his grip on her arms and stepped back, hooded lids concealing his eyes from her.

"After that, don't pretend that we have nothing more meaningful to discuss than the superficial trivia we exchanged downstairs," he said roughly, lifting one hand to comb it impatiently through the thick blackness of his hair.

The movement caught the light and something glinted on Nic's finger. Cathy felt suddenly sick as she realized what it was. A wedding ring.

Her throat felt tight and painful. "What would you like us to discuss then? Your marriage perhaps . . . your wife?"

Nic's eyes narrowed. "My what?"

"That is a wedding ring on your finger, I presume."

He glanced briefly at his hand and then thrust it deep into his trouser pocket, as though to hide the incriminating evidence. When he spoke there was the same biting anger of before. "It is a wedding ring. But my marriage is not a subject I have any wish to discuss with you."

Cathy's heart twisted painfully inside her. So Nic was married after all. Of course, she'd known it was possible... probable even... but somehow nothing had prepared her for the piercing agony of discovering it was a fact.

Her chin tilted, pride demanding that she should hide her dismayed reaction from him. "Whether you wish to discuss it or not doesn't matter. As far as I'm concerned you shouldn't be here and you certainly shouldn't be kissing me. I want you to go," she demanded.

Nic folded his arms. "I'm fascinated. Is this a display of moral scruples I am witnessing? What a pity they were not more in evidence five years ago."

"Stop it," she almost shrieked at him. "I don't know what game you're playing. I don't know why you keep talking about what happened five years ago—"

"I told you. I think you owe me an explanation!" Nic interrupted bitingly.

A burst of anger squared her shoulders. "Explanation? What sort of explanation do you expect? That I was young and naïve and inexperienced? You knew that, but it didn't make any difference to the way you treated me."

Nic's eyes narrowed. "The way *I* treated *you?*" He repeated her accusation disbelievingly. "*Dios!* What else did you expect? Surely you were not surprised by my reaction?"

Humiliation welled inside her. No, surprise was not the word to describe how she had felt that day. Stunned, bewildered, heartbroken, would be more accurate descriptions of her feelings. How would any woman feel on learning that the man she loved, her first and only lover, had found her a failure in bed and couldn't wait to see the back of her?

She shook her head and said brokenly, "I know you were...disappointed in me."

"Disappointed!" Nic rasped. "Is that all you think I was?"

Cathy's eyes grew wide. How could he be so cruel? "P-perhaps disappointed isn't the right word."

"No, it damn well isn't."

She turned away from him, struggling to regain control of herself. "It's over and done with, Nic. What's the point of raking it up after all this time?" She bit her lip. "I don't even think about it any more."

He raised one sceptical brow. "Lucky you, to sleep so easy in your bed." Then, seeing her colour, "Oh! Did I hit a raw nerve. Perhaps that was an unfortunate choice of words."

Cathy's fingers curled against her palms as she faced him. "I wouldn't call it unfortunate. I'd call it unforgivable."

Nic stared at her long and hard, his eyes as black as coals. "Unforgiveable? After what you did, how dare you use that term to me?"

Some distant corner of her mind tried to fathom his meaning. Nic was talking as if *she* had wronged him in some way. Which was crazy.

The tapping on the door behind her nearly made her jump out of her skin. She swung round to open the door.

"Ah, Signora Walker. I am Signora Rossi, the hotel manageress. I just came to see if everything was alright. Signor Lucciano brought some tablets for your migraine some time ago. He hasn't returned and I was worried that perhaps your condition was worse than you had indicated."

Cathy swallowed, pulling the door open wider to reveal Nic's presence in her bedroom. "I...thank you. How thoughtful of you. Ni—Signor Lucciano is still here."

La Signora Rossi's eyes narrowed slightly and Cathy thought her smile was a little forced. "Nicolas! I see you are looking after our guest."

By nearly giving me a heart attack, Cathy thought desperately. "Signor Lucciano was just about to leave," she said pointedly.

La Signora Rossi looked across the room at Nic. "Well, if you are sure we can do nothing else for you."

Cathy held the door open a little wider so Nic really didn't have much choice but to follow La Signora Rossi out.

Two

Far too distracted by the events of the night before, it had been an effort to make even the most desultory scribbles from time to time during the morning cooking demonstration.

By twelve-thirty, the rest of the group had departed by coach for the National Wine Library at Siena and Cathy was back at the hotel for lunch.

She quickly located a small table and ordered her food, spreading her notes on the table alongside her plate and staring down at them, trying to force her mind to concentrate on them. But it was no good. They simply blurred into an illegible mass before her eyes.

Instead her wilful thoughts returned time and again to that last fated visit to Florence. How different Nic had been then.

After only a couple of days in Italy, Harry had developed an upset stomach—probably the same bug his secretary had come down with, he surmised—and was confined to bed. He'd suggested that Cathy should go with Nic to visit the proposed hotel sites, make a few preliminary notes and that he would do the final inspection himself when he was feeling better.

A morning inspecting a hotel site with Nic had been followed by an afternoon exploring Pisa, followed by dinner. It had set the pattern for their days.

At first Cathy had been worried that Harry might complain that she wasn't getting enough work done. But Harry had seemed delighted when she told him Nic was taking her out. He'd actually told her to enjoy herself, making her feel a little guilty for all the uncharitable thoughts she'd harboured towards him in the past.

Time ran into itself and afterwards seemed only a brilliant kaleidoscope dominated by the intensely passionate sensation of falling in love.

She'd been involved with few men in her life... none really. When she was fifteen, her father had walked out on her and her mother very suddenly. There'd been no explanation, no discussion, he'd simply gone. She had blamed herself and been convinced that she must have disappointed him in some way. She'd never plucked up the courage to voice her fears and suddenly it was too late. He had died in a car accident when she was seventeen. Deep down fear of rejection always remained. Even as a teenager, she'd been wary of involvement... always fearing another rejection.

Until she met Nic, that is. He made her feel attractive and desirable... a woman worthy of being loved.

The last evening she'd spent in Italy had been the most romantic of her life. By the time they were driving back to Castel di Bellano in Nic's open-topped Mercedes, beneath a sky dotted with a million stars, she'd felt sublimely happy, drunk on champagne and love, mainly on love. When Nic drew her into his arms, she'd melted against the hard length of his body.

"*Dios!* I want you," Nic murmured huskily against the soft skin of her throat.

"I want you too," Cathy whispered, her body arching against his, her senses on fire.

Their journey upstairs and along the corridor was punctuated by kisses and caresses. By the time they reached Nic's bedroom her body was racked by shivers of desire.

Nic undressed her slowly and sensuously. Her blood seemed to grow hot. She returned his deepening kisses, shyly trying to imitate his arousing caresses as he stretched his naked form alongside hers.

Despite her arousal though, she couldn't prevent the sudden recoil which convulsed her muscles when Nic first entered her or fail to hear his muffled groan as he realized the reason for it, but by then it was too late. She was ready... more than ready... as she arched against him, her untutored body urging him to carry her on to sensations she'd never experienced before... destinations she'd never glimpsed before... and finally to a peak of wonder she'd never imagined before.

Later, much later, when she at last opened her eyes, she found Nic staring pensively into the darkness.

"Why didn't you tell me you were a virgin?"

The stark tone of the question made it sound as if she'd done something wrong and instinctively she tensed. "Does it matter?"

Nic expelled a ragged breath. "I hadn't realized you were so... inexperienced."

In the darkness, Cathy felt herself blushing. "W-was it so obvious?" The beautiful dreams she had been weaving in her head came crashing down to earth.

Nic's mouth hardened. "You're so young. *Dios!* Not even out of your teens. You know nothing of men."

Or men's needs. He didn't need to say it aloud for her to know that was really what he was talking about. The experience they had just shared might have been satisfying in every sense for her but obviously it hadn't been the same for him.

"You didn't enjoy making love with me, did you?" she said in a small voice.

A groan rumbled in Nic's throat. One lean finger came up to trace the curve of her cheek and he said softly. "You really are an innocent, aren't you, Cathy? Are the workings of men's bodies such a mystery to you?"

She frowned. Had the ultimate, climactic pleasure been hers alone? She felt an utter failure as a woman.

"I'm sorry," she whispered in a small voice.

"Don't be," Nic told her with a ragged sigh. "I should have known you'd never slept with a man before."

"And if you'd known, it wouldn't have happened. Is that what you're saying?"

"Go to sleep," he urged, not unkindly.

And there she had her answer, Cathy thought desolately. If he'd known she was a virgin, he wouldn't have made love to her. She felt as she had done when she was fifteen years old, lying wide-eyed in her bed, trying to work out what she could have done to stop her father leaving her.

She felt as if she was awake for hours but eventually she must have slept for when she awoke in the morning, Nic was no longer there.

Feeling more alone and dejected than she had ever done in her life, she slipped on a robe and left the room.

By unfortunate timing, Harry stepped out of his bedroom just as she was closing Nic's door behind her. He gave no indication of having seen her and Cathy exhaled a small sigh of relief. She didn't think she could face anyone this morning without bursting into tears.

She stayed in her room, half expecting Nic to come to her there. When it got to after nine o'clock, she knew he and Harry must have left for the city. Negotiations between them were in the final stages.

She was stunned when Harry arrived back at Castel di Bellano mid-morning and marched into the library where she was sitting with a thunderous expression on his face.

"You've messed things up well and truly this time," he informed her furiously by way of greeting. "You and Mr. Nicolas bloody Lucciano! He's called the deal off. And it's all because of you."

Blood drained from Cathy's face. Oh no! Surely Nic wouldn't have backed out of the contract with Harry just because... because she'd disappointed him in bed.

She swallowed hard, squashing down the awful possibility. "I'll talk to Nic. There must—"

Harry's face turned an even deeper shade of red. "No! He doesn't want to see you again. He wants us both gone from Castel di Bellano by the time he gets home this evening."

Cathy felt as if the world was spinning crazily. This couldn't be happening. Cathy wanted to scream and release the agonising denial building up inside her against everything Harry was saying but no sound came. She'd been rejected by Nic just as she'd been rejected by her father.

Like someone in a dream, she'd packed her bags and accompanied Harry to the airport.

"All alone?"

Cathy almost jumped out of her skin as the white, wrought iron chair opposite her own was scraped back and

Nic eased himself into it. "Yes," she spluttered. "And I don't want company."

"That's hardly polite," Nic observed coolly.

"Politeness?" Cathy retorted, her spirit invigorated by the bitter recollections of a few moments ago. "I thought we'd established very clearly last night that we can't stand each other."

Two black brows rose. "Is that what we established? When I kissed you I could have sworn that your response was not one of physical aversion."

Cathy willed the tide of scarlet which threatened to wash over her to remain at bay. "Don't flatter yourself, Nic."

"So your response would not be as enthusiastic if I were to kiss you a second time?"

My God! He was a married man. How dared he talk so casually about kissing her again? Once was bad enough.

"Certainly not," she said coldly. "Like most women, I despise cheating husbands."

Nic's expression suddenly darkened. "I'm a widower," he said tautly. "My wife died two years ago."

That stark announcement hit Cathy with all the impact of a brick. She stared at Nic, stunned by what he'd just told her. "I—I'm sorry," she said inadequately.

"Are you?"

"Of course I am," she insisted and meant it. "Why didn't you tell me this last night?" she asked, her voice softening a little.

"But then you would not have had the excuse of demanding that I leave, would you?"

"Now just a minute," Cathy said sharply, sensing that their temporary truce was about to come to an abrupt end. "Married or not, I didn't want you in my bedroom. I thought I'd made that clear. Now...if you'll excuse me," she said, pointedly smoothing out the sheets of paper with her notes on them. "I do have some work to do. I'm being paid to do a job here, not idle my time away in conversation with you."

Suddenly Nic's mouth curved in a hard smile. "Yet once I think you were paid to idle your time away in just such a manner, albeit rather more charmingly."

She frowned. "What do you mean?"

"How is Harry?" Nic enquired softly, ignoring her question.

A small shiver ran down Cathy's spine. Why was he asking her about Harry? Even thinking about Harry made her shudder.

After returning from Italy five years ago, Cathy had been full of pain. When a friend had asked if she wanted a summer job with a small catering business specializing in directors' lunches and private functions, she'd been glad to have something . . . anything to fill her time.

She'd even been grateful when Harry offered to put some work their way. Until Harry suddenly mentioned a small, private directors' lunch and presented her with a small tape recorder, telling her to hide it somewhere under the table before the guests arrived.

"The company's ripe for a takeover," he'd explained, "And it's amazing what information is let slip over lunch. Everyone does it."

"Not me," Cathy had told him furiously.

Shortly afterwards she had left home and started flat sharing with Graham, a friend from school days. Cathy had never trusted Harry again.

"He's well, I think. I don't see him and my mother very often," she told Nic carefully now.

"Why not?"

Cathy moistened her lips with her tongue. "Our paths just don't often cross, that's all. I have a full-time job—"

"Ah! Yes...your job. Was Harry responsible for getting you that?"

"No, he wasn't," Cathy spluttered in angry denial.

Nic's eyes were like chips of ice. "I merely thought that one good turn might have deserved another. After all, you have done favours for Harry in the past." Nic's black gaze pinned her in her seat. "Sleeping with me for one."

Cathy blinked several times, certain she must have misheard him. "What are you talking about?" she whispered.

"Oh, come on, Cathy. Don't play the innocent," Nic derided cruelly. His rage was like a physical force assaulting her across the table. "Cannot you yet admit the truth? That you and Harry tried to set me up."

Cathy's heart was thudding so wildly that she was sure Nic must be able to hear it. "Set you up? How?" Cathy was lost in a maze of utter confusion.

"Harry told me the truth," Nic said bluntly. "He was too full of blind anger to lie. He told me how you had agreed to sleep with me in return for certain financial remuneration when the deal was successfully completed."

Cathy gazed at him across the table in complete and utter dismay. "Harry told you *that?*"

Nic's eyes narrowed to two black slits of smouldering fury. "Oh! Not quite as coolly as I have repeated it now...nor quite so politely. It was the morning we were due to sign the contracts," Nic said tautly. "The terms had already been agreed, but Harry wanted to make some last minute changes. Changes that were, needless to say, advantageous to him and disadvantageous to me." His mouth twisted in distaste. "Evidently he assumed that you and I had enjoyed such a night of unbridled passion that I would agree to them.''

Blood was thundering through Cathy's head at a hundred miles an hour. She shook her head. ''But how did Harry know we'd spent the night together?''

''Exactly.''

She remembered now. He must have seen her leave Nic's bedroom on that last morning, after all. She felt suddenly sick.

''Evidently Harry did not know me very well,'' Nic continued. ''He failed to realize that I despise people who agree to terms and then try to twist them to suit themselves . . . just as I despise women who sleep with men for material gain.''

Cathy felt imminently close to tears. ''You can't really think that!'' she cried painfully. ''I was a virgin . . . you knew that.''

''Virginity can be viewed as a disposable commodity like anything else.''

Cathy gasped at him in horror. A disposable commodity! ''Don't you dare say that to me. He used both of us, can't you see that? When he realized he wasn't going to get his own way, he got nasty. He knew it would hurt your pride if he told you I'd only slept with you because he'd offered me money. He wounded your vanity, that was all. Perhaps you should be grateful that that was all he hurt.''

With that, Cathy stood up and scraped her chair back from the table. She paid no attention to the curious looks of the other diners as, head held high, she marched away.

Three

Cathy walked and walked until she was exhausted. By the time she got back to the hotel, it was nearly dusk. She made her way straight up to her room and minutes later was lying back in a hot, deep bath, eyes closed.

How could Nic have believed her capable of such ugly deceit and trickery? But why was it so shocking that Nic had believed Harry when she'd been so completely taken in too? Cathy reminded herself abruptly.

Hearing a tap on her bedroom door, Cathy got out of the bath, pulled on a towelling robe and padded through to the bedroom.

"Who is it?" she called, intuition providing the answer before any response could be made.

"Nic!"

"What do you want?"

"To talk to you." An exasperated sound came from the other side of the door. "Now will you please open this door or do I have to do something drastic?"

Cathy stared apprehensively at the wooden panelling. He surely wouldn't break the door down. He just might, an inner voice warned her.

Trembling fingers reached for the lock and released it. She instinctively stepped back as Nic came into the room.

Whatever he'd been about to say was stifled on a ragged breath as his gaze took in her towelled covering and the damp tendrils of chestnut hair that curled wildly about her shoulders.

Nic's dark eyes ran appreciatively over her as he murmured, half to himself, "Five years ago you were a beautiful girl. Now you are a beautiful woman."

Beautiful! What did that mean? A pleasing composition of face and figure. Nothing more. As for being a woman...what sort of woman was it who couldn't satisfy a man in bed?

Cathy forced herself to hold his gaze, not to betray the inner wave of mortification she felt. "I'm sure you didn't come here simply to feed me compliments, Nic. You said you wanted to talk. What about?"

His black eyes settled on her face. "You can ask that so glibly after our exchange at lunch-time?"

"I'm not sure you even believe what I told you at lunch-time."

"Neither am I." Nic watched her closely, eyes narrowing. "If this is so, why did you not stay and tell me the truth five years ago?"

"Stay? You didn't give me an opportunity. You ordered me out of Castel di Bellano, remember?"

Nic frowned. "Ordered you out of Castel di Bellano! What are you talking about?"

"When Harry came back, he told me you wanted him and me to leave straight away...that you didn't want to find me there when you got home that evening."

Nic muttered an expletive under his breath. "And you believed him?"

A lump seemed to be forming in Cathy's throat. Already mortified by what had happened the night before, she'd needed little persuasion to believe that what Harry said must be true.

"Harry was so angry...so convincing," she offered jerkily. Confused thoughts whizzed through Cathy's mind. If Nic hadn't wanted her to go, why had he refused to take her phone calls? "But I tried to phone you from England. You wouldn't even speak to me. All I got was an icy rebuff from your secretaries every time I tried to get through to you."

Nic shook his head. "When I discovered that you had left Florence with Harry that day, without making any attempt to contact me, it all pointed to only one possible conclusion. That you were as guilty as Harry had said. I was so furious that I resolved there and then to have no further communication with you."

Cathy's hand flew to her mouth. "Harry wanted to get me out of the way before you could speak to me...he knew if we saw each other his lies would be blown wide open."

"So it seems," Nic agreed bitterly. "But you had made love with me only that night. How could you have believed that I would send you away in such a callous manner?"

Cathy swallowed, her throat tight. "Didn't it occur to you that I felt very..." she paused, searching for a suitable word, "...very awkward by what had happened when we made love?"

"Awkward?"

Oh God! He wasn't just making this difficult, he was making it impossible. Her control felt at knife edge. "Yes, awkward," she snapped tightly. "You were obviously disappointed in me. I knew I hadn't exactly satisfied you as...as a lover."

A ragged breath was punched from Nic's throat. "*Dios!* Don't tell me you believed I wanted you gone because of that?"

"Of course that's what I believed," Cathy retorted sharply, hiding her hurt at having such painfully intimate memories exposed.

Nic's eyes darkened briefly on her face and there was a moment's silence before he said more quietly, "I have no excuse for that. I should have put the brakes on when I realized what was happening but I didn't. Once I knew you were a virgin, I was disgusted with myself for taking advantage of you." His mouth hardened. "It wasn't *you* I was angry with. It was myself."

Why didn't that admission make her feel better, Cathy wondered bleakly? Perhaps because she didn't truly believe it. Not that she thought Nic was lying. But the fact remained that their lovemaking had been a dismal failure from his point of view. There was no getting away from that.

"Anyway," she murmured, trying to sound indifferent. "It hardly matters, does it? We're different people now. Things have changed. You've been ... married ..."

Her throat contracted with the pain of thinking of Nic married to another woman, a woman whom he must have loved very much, a woman who had no doubt satisfied him fully in every way.

Nic's fingers cupped her chin, and her heart began to thud wildly.

"What's the matter? Why are you crying?" he demanded.

"I'm not," Cathy denied, blinking hard. He was far too close, far too overwhelming to her senses.

"Yes, you are." Slowly he drew her towards him, one arm sliding round her waist. His mouth found hers, infinitely skilful, infinitely sensual, grazing the soft inner flesh with his tongue. Blood thundered through her head. In five years no man had kissed her with this degree of intimacy...no man had come close to arousing this kind of response.

"Have dinner with me this evening."

Say no, every ounce of reason demanded. You know there can only be more pain in prolonging your time in his company.

"I can't."

"Can't or won't?"

"What would be the point, Nic? After all, all this happened a long time ago. You've been married and I..." She paused. She'd spent the last five years trying to fall out of love with Nic, not falling in love with anyone else!

"What's the harm in dinner? You're not frightened of being in my company, are you?"

"Why should I be?" Cathy bristled.

"I have no idea," Nic returned silkily.

Cathy felt as if she'd been backed into a corner. She took a deep breath. "There is no harm, I suppose," she admitted grudgingly.

"Eight o'clock then."

Before she could make any reply whatsoever, Nic had completed the arrangements and was gone. Once he left, she leaned back against the door and closed her eyes. Why on earth had she agreed? She really couldn't believe she'd done such a foolish thing.

Four

Throughout the meal she and Nic had talked of subjects which were personal without being intimate...Cathy's work, Nic's business, the restorations he was making to Castel di Bellano. Amidst the candle-lit surroundings and with soft music playing in the background, such exchanges came easily enough but all the while she was conscious of a tension flickering like electricity between them.

"More wine?" He lifted the bottle enquiringly.

Cathy shook her head. She felt quite drunk enough already and it had nothing to do with the couple of glasses of wine she'd had with the meal.

Nic filled his own glass and the candlelight caught the glint of the gold band on his left hand.

Cathy felt that same jolt of pain she had done on the previous night when she had first seen it. Nic was wearing another woman's ring on his wedding finger and, even knowing he was a widower, that still hurt.

"How long were you married?" she asked quietly.

"Two years."

Cathy's heart tightened. Two years! If his wife had died two years ago, that must mean they'd married less than a year after she left Italy. It hadn't taken him long to meet someone else and fall in love. She really had only ever been a one-night stand in his eyes, hadn't she?

It was torture to ask more and yet still she couldn't stop herself. "Was your wife Italian?"

"Yes, she was. Now do you think we could drop this subject?" Nic said tautly. "My wife is not a subject I wish to discuss. I thought I had made that clear."

The transformation in his manner was so abrupt that Cathy almost flinched in shock. He must have loved her deeply for his grief to still be so raw.

"I'm sorry," she said. "I couldn't help noticing that you still wear your wedding ring," she offered by way of explanation for her intrusive comments.

Nic glanced at the band of gold on his finger. "Yes," he agreed shortly. "I find it useful . . . it serves as a reminder."

"Of your wife?"

"Of my marriage."

There was a subtle difference but Cathy wasn't allowed to dwell on it sufficiently to fathom it as Nic asked, "Would you care to dance?" He hardly waited for her nodded response before taking her hand in his and drawing her on to the small dance floor.

A slow number was playing and he immediately drew her into his arms as if it was the most natural thing in the world.

His body was lean and hard as it brushed against hers, sensitizing every skin cell with the contact. Being this close to him was like some form of exquisite torture which frightened and intoxicated her simultaneously. Her body was responding to Nic's with all the wild, heady abandon it had done five years ago. The same spreading heat, the quickening pulse, the ragged breathing, the painful tugging deep inside her. It frightened her.

"I heard you were living with someone. Is it true?"

That coolly delivered question almost had Cathy's legs buckling beneath her. He must mean Graham, she guessed instantly. He thought she and Graham were living together. As lovers!

"Who told you that?" she demanded, completely thrown by the unexpected question.

"It doesn't matter who. Is it true?"

Stung by the blatant unfairness of Nic asking such personal questions of her when he'd refused point blank to discuss his own private life, Cathy gave him an impatient look. "I suppose it doesn't occur to you that I might not want to discuss this with *you?*"

"I'm not asking for details. A simple yes or no will suffice."

Did she really want him to know how emotionally barren the last five years had been for her? All she had to do was let him think that she and Graham had lived together as lovers.

"I...I was living with someone but w-we're no longer together," she said. The last bit was true at least. Now that Graham had moved in with Cassie, Cathy and he were no longer living together.

"When did you break up?"

"A—a few months ago."

The music stopped and Nic released his hold on her. Cathy risked a swift glance at his face but in the candlelight it was impossible to decipher his expression.

Later, when she stepped out of Nic's car outside the hotel, Cathy couldn't suppress a slight shiver.

"Are you cold?"

"A little," she nodded and then felt awkward when Nic slid off his jacket and draped it round her shoulders.

When they reached the lift in the reception area, Cathy went to remove the jacket and hand it back to Nic with a polite thank you, for both its loan and the meal. But to her consternation, he promptly stepped into the empty lift with her, casually instructing, "Keep it on until you get to your room."

The lift felt far too small and claustrophobic and Cathy's heart was thumping so loudly that she was sure Nic was able to hear it.

His fingers curved on her shoulders and drew her against him. It was what she'd been terrified of. Nic's breath fanned her cheek and his mouth found hers.

It wasn't a gentle, exploring kiss. It was explosively possessive as his tongue thrust into the moist recess of her mouth, making her lips fall open beneath his. A hot fire sparked in the pit of her stomach and the blood was pounding at breathtaking speed through her body. She felt a moan hover in the soft hollow of her throat and then seek its release against the exquisite hardness of Nic's mouth.

Oh God! She should put a stop to this madness right now. It was crazy, utterly crazy. How could she behave like this, like a wanton? she demanded feverishly of herself.

When the lift stopped, she flung Nic's jacket at him and stepped out into the corridor, overwhelmingly relieved to find it empty.

Instantly he grabbed her wrist and yanked her back to face him. "Cathy, what happened just now—"

"Should never have happened," she snapped, avoiding his eyes.

"Why not?"

Her throat felt tight and sore. "Don't pretend. You know as well as I do that what we were doing wasn't going to stop at a few kisses."

"And if it didn't, what's wrong with that?"

He *knew* how disastrous it had been last time. But probably he thought she was more sexually experienced now... more likely to understand the techniques of pleasing a man in bed.

"Everything's wrong with it," she bit back at him, wishing he would just turn around and walk away from her. But his tall, powerful body filled the corridor, making her feel like a trapped animal. "You've been married," she ground out in desperation.

"I'm not married now, I'm widowed," he revised coolly. "So that makes us both unattached..." He paused, his black eyes narrowing on her face. "...Or aren't you unattached? Are you still involved with this man, Graham?"

Why did he keep asking whether she was involved with anyone? Cathy thought as the blood pounded through her head, making rational thought impossible.

They had reached her bedroom door and she slotted her key in the lock, using those precious few seconds to compose her face before swinging round to face him. She forced her voice to sound hard and brittle although she felt as if she was breaking into thousands of little pieces inside.

"You didn't really believe it was *you* I wanted in the lift, did you? Quite honestly I wanted a man. Any man. I told you Graham left me some months ago. Since then my... er...physical needs haven't been fulfilled and just now sexual frustration got the better of me, that's all."

She knew what Nic would do now. He would turn and walk away from her and she would never see him again. Her heart felt as if it would shatter at the prospect. She was deeply ashamed of herself for lying so callously but if this hurt, how much more would it hurt to have to watch him walk away *after* he had made love to her? She couldn't bear that kind of rejection again.

Somehow she managed to lift her eyes up to meet his at last and encountered a face almost black with rage.

"*Dios!* You little bitch," he derided furiously. "So you want a man, do you? Well I've always believed in giving a woman what she wants. Only tonight, *cara,* you'll know it isn't any man in your bed. You'll know it's me."

Cathy was so shocked that she stepped back jerkily through the open doorway and into her room.

"What do you mean?" she demanded wildly.

"Precisely what I say," he assured her, kicking the door shut with his foot.

Cathy stared at him in alarm. Her lips felt as dry as parchment as she ran her tongue over them. "Nic, I'm sorry, I shouldn't have said what I did," she stumbled hurriedly over her apology. "I don't know what came over me."

Nic folded his arms and surveyed her, his expression closed and unrelenting. "Sexual frustration, you said," he offered derisively, one hand snaking out to circle her wrist and pull her towards him. "Tonight, *cara,* I do not want any ghosts in your head or in your bed. The only man with you will be me. Do you understand?"

Cathy felt as if she was being hypnotised. Nic's thumb was rubbing the inside of her wrist in slow, erotic circles, quickening her blood flow. He lifted her hand to his mouth and ran his teeth the length of her thumb before taking it into his mouth and sucking it slowly and deliberately.

All the time, his eyes never left hers, watching the play of emotions shimmering in their green depths.

She didn't know which was worse. His rage of a few moments ago or this detached display of sexual expertise.

"Please don't," she heard herself saying and thought how ineffectual it sounded. A token protest, nothing more.

"Don't you like me touching you?" Nic enquired softly. What was the point of further lies? He knew the effect he was having on her. "You know I do," she murmured, biting back the moan which trembled in her throat.

Nic bent his head to touch her lips with his, teasing them apart with slow, leisurely movements. "Then why are you asking me to stop?" he drawled huskily.

Dear God! She didn't know any more. Desire gripped her as forcefully as any vice, possessing her body in its inescapable grasp.

"Do you want me to stop?"

"No. . . no," she whispered. Shocked by the abandon of her own thoughts, Cathy's eyes flew open and locked momentarily with Nic's. Startled green clashed with black. What could she see there? Victory?

But the expression she saw in his eyes was almost more shocking than that. He wants me! He really wants me, she thought, heart pounding madly. She reached out to touch him, hands flattening on the muscled wall of chest through the silk shirt. His skin felt warm and powerful beneath her fingers and she was amazed by the sudden shuddering response her touch provoked.

His lovemaking was no longer the cool delivery of a refined skill, intended to punish her for her cruel taunts, but a raw expression of his need.

Unerringly his fingers moved to the clasp at the back of her dress, releasing it so that the bodice fell in silky folds about her waist, exposing her swollen breasts.

"Oh!" Cathy gasped as Nic's mouth closed over one taut nipple, making it tighten and throb with piercing pleasure. Her neck arched back and the pins loosened in her hair, sending a mass of gold red curls tumbling over her shoulders. Her fingers went to the buttons of his shirt, releasing them with awkward, fumbling tugs, even pulling some of the buttons off altogether.

With a briefly amused look, Nic helped her then, slipping the shirt from his shoulders and tossing it to some distant corner of the room.

His skin was warm and the male aroma which clung to it tantalisingly erotic. Her touch grew bolder, nails scoring the powerful wall of chest and closing on the taut nub she located there.

Tension rippled through Nic's body and Cathy felt the unmistakable leap of hard muscle between his thighs. Her eyes opened to find him watching her, an odd expression on his face.

What was he feeling right now? Guilt? Was he thinking that it shouldn't have been her in his arms but the wife he had lost?

Her body suddenly felt as if it had been coated in ice and she stiffened in his arms. "I—I can't do this," she told him brokenly.

He stared at her, his eyes suddenly cold and questioning. "Because of this man you were living with?"

Just say yes, she told herself bleakly. You've woven so many deceits round Graham already. What does one more matter? It's less painful for everyone that way. She swallowed and nodded. "That's right."

Nic just kept right on looking at her, tension crackling in the air between them. Her dress pooled around her feet to reveal creamy silk briefs, her only underwear.

He groaned hoarsely, eyes darkening as they swept low over the rounded curve of her hips and lower still to the triangle of red gold curls, clearly visible beneath the transparent wisp of silk.

Cathy had thought he was about to cast her from him in furious rejection but instead his fingers closed on her arms and he pushed her backwards onto the bed.

"I told you, *cara*, tonight there will be only one man in your bed and that man will be me."

As she watched him in mounting dismay, his fingers went to the waistband of his trousers, released the fastening and stripped them off. The rest of his clothing followed in a matter of seconds until he stood before her, starkly and magnificently naked.

A wave of heated desire swept over her. Had she forgotten how superbly male he was? Or had she simply blocked that visual memory out along with so many others?

Say something, her tortured brain instructed. Tell him to stop. He will stop this madness if you tell him to.

His gaze swept over her naked body. "You're beautiful," he murmured roughly. "So beautiful..."

Cathy's eyes snapped shut as his mouth covered hers in a searing kiss which left her gasping for breath. His fingers stroked her body with unbelievable patience, tracing the valley between her breasts, the smooth plane of her abdomen, the gentle curve of her thighs, over and over again until her body was on fire.

"Please, Nic," she murmured breathlessly against his mouth.

In an incredible erotic gesture, his tongue circled the inner softness of her lips. "This isn't enough, huh, *cara*?" he drawled huskily. "You want more?"

"Yes...yes," she gasped, eyes locking with his.

His gaze darkened and his hand roamed lower, sending her body into abandoned tremors of delight, making her arch to meet the questing fingers which were exploring her so intimately.

A shaft of cool air feathered her skin as Nic abruptly levered himself upright. "You are protected, aren't you?"

Contraception! She'd never even thought of it, Cathy realized guiltily. In fact, she was on the pill but not for the reason he obviously assumed. It was to regulate her periods, nothing more.

She swallowed and nodded, expecting him to be glad to be relieved of the responsibility but instead his jaw tightened and he looked almost angry. Was it possible that Nic was jealous at the thought of her sleeping with another man?

His probing tongue and roaming fingers were setting her body alight once more, making her squirm beneath his in pleasure. Every muscle in her was getting tighter, every inch of skin hotter, every nerve screaming for release. Her fingers were clutching at Nic's body in desperate snatches.

Was it the same for him too? she wondered feverishly. This incredible sensation of urgency and tormented longings?

"Nic, please…do you…is it the same…" She stumbled raggedly over the words.

For a moment Nic stopped and stared at her, his eyes darkening on her face, then he seemed to understand the meaning behind her incoherent words.

"Dios!" He grated raggedly. "Do you still need reassurance of what you do to me? Do you still not know?"

Slowly, his eyes not leaving hers, his hands circled her hips, drawing her against the hard, muscled evidence of his own need, and then sliding deep inside her, whispering husky, erotic reassurances all the time.

Cathy had never imagined that anything could be such sweet torture. Her head arched back as her body took up the rhythm, each thrusting stroke bringing her closer and closer to the brink of ecstasy, each grinding intimacy a step further on this incredible... amazing trip to the edge of the world.

Suddenly she was being catapulted into a star-dazzled universe and her body was spinning round and round, dazedly, wonderfully out of control.

She could hear her own voice moaning... hear Nic's raw groan of satisfaction... feel the intense waves of pleasure pulsing through her... before her muscles relaxed and she felt his arms close possessively around her.

Five

Cathy woke to sunshine filtering in through the open window. The crumpled pillow beside her own had long since grown cold.

One thing for sure, she knew it hadn't been a dream. The unfamiliar tenderness of certain parts of her body told her that. Had that panting, trembling woman who had lain in Nic's arms last night really been her?

The same woman who'd scored his back with her nails as she urged him to her...moaned her pleasure out loud...heard his own raw groan of satisfaction?

Despite all her misgivings, she *knew* that Nic had taken as much fulfilment from their love-making as she had...and how joyous it felt to discover at last that she was as capable of giving pleasure as taking it.

Impulsively, she longed to tell him how she felt...but Nic had obviously left during the early hours of the morning. She felt a piercing stab of disappointment. Why hadn't he woken her before he went?

What a stupid question! Colour flooded her cheeks as she recalled the bitter taunts she'd flung at him at her bedroom door.

She must speak to him . . . and say what? That she'd told him a pack of lies, that there were no other lovers? What purpose would such confessions serve? As far as he was concerned, they'd been just two *adults* spending the night together. This wasn't like last time. Then she'd at least *thought* he loved her. This time she *knew* he didn't. He'd lost the woman he loved, the woman who'd been his wife.

Frowning unhappily, Cathy swung her legs over the side of the bed and walked over to the en-suite bathroom. She spent ages in the shower, her thoughts a twisted mass of contradictions. Part of her wanted to revel in the womanly sensations which filled her and part of her wanted to wash away every trace of the night which had just passed. Each sunny burst of joy was quickly stifled by the knowledge that Nic had left...without a word, without even leaving a note.

Unless...the thought suddenly occurred to her...he had left a note or a message at the reception when he left.

She dried herself at lightning speed, tugged on a pair of white cotton jeans, teaming them with a blue and white T-shirt and white loafers, then picked up her bag, locked the door and almost ran down the stairs two at a time.

She asked the receptionist if there were any messages for her and her heart did a tattoo when a white sheet of paper was passed to her.

But it was only a telephone message from Graham, warning her that several large items of furniture, wedding presents from various guests, were being delivered to the flat during her absence.

She folded the paper up, grateful for Graham's thoughtfulness in letting her know but unconcerned right now about how cluttered the flat became with his and Cassie's wedding presents. All she could think of was that Nic had walked out on her without a word. She tried to swallow the huge lump building in her throat.

"Mi sembra che ci sia un errore," she suggested, hoping against hope that there may be another note.

The receptionist obligingly checked again. *"Mi 'spiace,"* she shrugged apologetically.

On another day, learning how to make the Livorno version of *baccala,* salt cod with tomatoes, garlic and black olives, might have held her attention but today it had no chance. Cathy could hardly wait for the morning's classes to be over so that she could get back to the hotel and see if there were any messages from Nic.

But when she arrived, she was once again bitterly disappointed. No notes, no messages.

If he really didn't intend to contact her, what could she do? She could do what she'd done last time. Believe the worst and flee Italy without daring to confront him...or she could go and see him herself.

She asked the receptionist to call her a taxi. If she was going to act, she knew she had to do it now before her courage failed her.

The day was glorious, and the approach to Castel di Bellano was just as beautiful as Cathy remembered. When she rounded a corner and saw it towering before her, its tower and minarets turning to burnt sienna in the sunlight, she let out a small gasp of pleasure.

As the taxi drew into the gravelled forecourt area, the first thing she saw was Nic's black Mercedes parked there. He must be at home then, she thought, an odd mixture of excitement and apprehension building inside her. He wouldn't be expecting to see her. Would he be pleased or annoyed?

Perhaps she shouldn't be so nervous but she was, Cathy realized. Her stomach was winding itself into knots. If she didn't get out of the car quickly, she might ask the taxi driver to drive straight on and take her back to the hotel.

She paid the man quickly and stepped out of the taxi. As he drove away, she noticed a small boy playing with a bucket, his whole attention focused on filling it with tiny chips of gravel. En route to the main door, she paused to say hello, thinking what a gorgeous child he was with his silky dark hair and huge lustrous eyes. He stared solemnly at Cathy and then smiled, so beautifully that it was like the sun coming out on a miserable November day in London. Cathy couldn't help but smile back.

She raised her head at the sound of voices, her smile fading as Nic appeared round the corner of the castle in faded denims and a white T-shirt which hugged his muscled chest revealingly. His eyes were hooded as they surveyed her.

Cathy swallowed, knowing instinctively that Nic wasn't just surprised to see her—he was shocked and angry. He muttered something to the woman at his side who immediately called to the child. The little boy toddled across to her, taking her hand as she led him into the castle.

He doesn't want to see me, Cathy thought on a black wave of despair. She knew she had to say something but she couldn't even begin to think of any of the things she'd intended to say.

"He's gorgeous, isn't he?" she said with a falsely bright air, gesturing in the direction the little boy had gone.

Nic made no move to speak or bridge the distance between them. On God! Why did I ever come? Cathy thought.

"Is he that woman's son?" she asked, for want of anything better to say.

"No," Nic said at last. "He's mine."

Cathy felt as if she had just been hit. *No, he's mine.* The shocking words pounded through her head over and over again. She clutched a hand to her mouth.

"What are you doing here?" Nic demanded jaggedly.

"Why didn't you tell me you had a child?" she retorted wildly.

"Don't answer a question with a question."

"I can't believe you didn't tell me you had a son," Cathy burst out, ignoring his reproof, her eyes turning to two shocked green pools in her face.

Nic's profile was set in harsh, unrelenting lines. "I didn't tell you because Luc's existence has nothing to do with you and me."

Nothing had prepared her for this. She had thought perhaps that he might be vexed at her unexpected arrival... even that he might be a little cool because of the awful things she had said to him. But she had not expected to find him so ruthlessly indifferent to her feelings, especially given this new discovery.

"How can you say that?" she demanded brokenly. "After last night, how can you say that?"

Hard, angry eyes stared down at her. "Last night we slept together, that's all," he returned derisively. "It doesn't entitle either of us to the personal details of each other's lives."

Every drop of colour drained from her face at that cruel rebuff. A one-night stand! Was that all it had been to him? "It should at least entitle both of us to honesty from the other," she replied with an attempt at dignity.

"Honesty?" Nic gave her a scathing look. "Oh! I would agree. It should do that. But I never *lied* to you, Cathy."

"You certainly kept your son's existence a secret." Cathy dashed the back of her wrist against her cheek, brushing away hot tears.

"It was not a secret. Simply a matter which I had no reason to discuss with you," Nic said tautly.

And that was supposed to make her feel better? His son's existence was *a matter* he'd had no reason to discuss with her? He could hardly have shown her more clearly how peripheral a slot she'd briefly occupied in his life.

"Why did you come here?" he repeated roughly.

All the things that she had planned to say to him seemed quite redundant now. He wasn't interested in hearing the truth about Graham . . . or anything else. He didn't care.

"I came to see you but I . . . I can see I shouldn't have done," Cathy returned brokenly. "It was a mistake. I realize that now. Don't worry. I won't stay."

His fingers caught her arm as she made to turn away. "You still haven't told me why you came."

"Isn't it obvious? I wanted to talk to you," Cathy retorted, struggling against the restraining grip of his fingers. "You'd gone when I woke this morning . . . you didn't leave any message . . . any note."

There was a moment's silence and then Nic's hard mouth twisted. "A thank-you note for being the one permitted to take your lover's place and relieve your *sexual frustration?*" Callously, he threw her own crude term of the night before back at her.

That taunt was too much for her ravaged emotions. Her hand rose instinctively towards his cheek but he grabbed it before it reached its target. "Is that term not to your liking in the harsh light of day?"

"It's not to my liking, day or night," she snapped.

"And yet last night I distinctly recall you telling me that's what you were suffering from," Nic grated harshly.

Oh God! Had he really believed her when she'd said that? Was that why he was being so cruel? "It wasn't true," she said fiercely. "Graham was not my lover. We're not even living together any more."

"No?"

"No!"

Cathy lifted her hands in a despairing gesture. "Please, Nic... last night I said some things which weren't true. Not because I wanted to deceive you... everything seemed to happen so quickly that I panicked. Can't you understand that? Surely you know that I... I wanted you to make love to me. I thought it was what we both wanted. I thought we both... enjoyed it."

Nic stared at her, his eyes darkening on her pleading expression. For a moment she thought she had reached him but then the moment was gone and his features had once again assumed their ice-cold mask.

"I did enjoy it. It was very satisfying," he assured her sardonically. "What more could a man wish for?"

Satisfying! He made it sound like a good meal in a restaurant. As if all they had been doing was assuaging an appetite. Was that really all it had been?

"If I hadn't come today, you wouldn't have contacted me, would you?" Cathy asked bleakly.

He stood watching her, hands on hips, observing the play of emotions on her face. "No," he agreed curtly. "There would have been no point."

Cathy swallowed. Dear God! He'd never intended to see her again. He'd just said as much.

"No, I suppose not," she agreed, struggling to keep the tremor from her voice. Her chin tilted and she said, with as much dignity as she could muster, "I hope you won't mind if I call a taxi."

"A taxi will not be necessary. I will drive you back. I owe you that at least." Nothing he could have said would have made her feel more like a whore.

Six

It wasn't until she was up and dressed the next morning that Cathy remembered there were no lectures or workshops that day. It was the one clear day, allowing all the course participants an opportunity to spend the day exactly as they wished: sightseeing, shopping, or simply relaxing.

Not that she was in the mood for any of those things. In fact, if it hadn't been for the fact that she was already up, she thought she might well have spent the day in bed, the curtains drawn and her face buried in a pillow.

A cynical smile tugged at the corners of her mouth. It wouldn't have been very comfortable. Her pillow was still damp from all the tears she'd shed since yesterday.

She felt sick inside every time she thought of the previous day's encounter with Nic. She could still hardly believe how cold and cruel his manner towards her had been. Had guilt driven him to such extremes? Did he feel that by sleeping with her he had somehow betrayed the wife he'd loved?

Cathy buried her face in her hands in a despairing gesture. She had to do something...anything. Just to stop herself going mad.

In the end, she decided to be like any other visitor to the city and do some shopping for small gifts to take home.

Cathy wandered at leisure along the central Via dei Calzaiuoli and Via dei Tornabuoni, where the city's smartest shops were situated, forcing herself to examine the chic fashion designs and elaborate leather goods on display although she knew perfectly well that her heart wasn't in it.

Nearly an hour later, her arms laden with packages, Cathy walked back to the hotel. She almost collided with someone emerging from the revolving doors at the entrance.

The flare of heat which engulfed her skin as strong hands settled on her shoulders warned her who the person was even before her eyes did. Nic!

His hands still rested on her shoulders and every fingertip seemed imprinted there. It took a deliberate effort of will on her part to twist slightly and release herself.

"Excuse me." She went to move into one of the empty door compartments, head bent in case he saw the sudden rush of weak tears to her eyes.

His hand came up to hold the door, preventing it turning. "You've been shopping, I see." He glanced at the packages in her arms.

"Yes," she said, almost defiantly, in reaction to the cutting edge she detected in his voice. What had he expected her to do? Sit in her room and wallow in misery?

"For your trousseau?"

That cynical taunt had her eyes widening in shock. Yesterday she'd thought he'd wounded her with every weapon at his disposal.

"Wouldn't a trousseau be a little previous since I haven't even booked a wedding yet?" she snapped, teeth clenching.

"No more previous than your guests sending you their wedding presents already."

This time Cathy could only stare at him in genuine confusion. "I really have no idea what you're talking about," she told him flatly.

"You did not receive your fiancé's message?"

What fiancé? What message? "Of course I didn't. I don't even have—"

"You don't perhaps remember Graham, your fiancé. The man you claimed you were not even living with any more," Nic snarled, his face only inches away from hers.

Cathy stepped back, stunned by the raw anger in his voice. Her mind whirled, trying to make sense of what he was saying. "This is ridiculous. Graham's not my fiancé. He's engaged to someone else."

"That's why he sends *you* messages about wedding presents being delivered to your flat, is it?"

Messages? Wedding presents? All at once lucidity tumbled in and Cathy realised that Nic must have seen Graham's message yesterday and thought *she* and Graham were going to be married. Of all the crazy...

"Because we used to share the flat... it still belongs to him. He's using it to store the larger wedding presents, that's all," she bit out.

They stared at each other, the tension between them almost visible. Nic shook his head and raked a hand roughly through his hair. "What are you saying? That you are not engaged to him?"

"Of course I'm not!" Did Nic really believe she could have slept with him if she was engaged to another man?

His next words indicated that was precisely what he did think. "When I saw that note, I assumed..."

"You assumed I'd lied to you about my relationship with Graham. You jumped to the conclusion that I was the kind of woman who would betray her fiancé by going to bed with another man. That's...that's disgusting." Eyes blurring with angry tears, she knocked his arm from the door and moved to enter it but his fingers falling on her shoulder held her fast.

Almost before Cathy realized what was happening, Nic was propelling her ahead of him through the door and into the hotel. His fingers clamped tightly on her arm as he guided her to a small office at the end of one of the corridors.

"Isn't kidnapping a criminal offence in Italy?" she gritted.

"Only when it is accompanied by demands for money. I am merely demanding a little of your time," he informed her. "I behaved badly yesterday—"

She twisted out of his grasp, tossing over her shoulder, "Badly? You didn't just behave badly. You made me feel like a whore."

His eyes darkened. "*Dios!* Do not say that!"

Cathy's eyes flashed emerald green. "Why not? It's true! You treated me like a woman you'd picked up on the streets. Except when you left, you didn't leave anything, did you? No note, no message, nothing."

A muscle clenched along Nic's jawline. "I was about to leave you a note...until I discovered another man's message had arrived for you."

He hadn't just intended it to be a one-night stand then! Cathy's heart gave a sudden leap but she quickly squashed her elated response. Whatever Nic had intended hardly mattered now, did it? "And reached your own conclusions," she reminded him tautly. "Without even speaking to me, you were ready to believe the very worst. That's what I don't understand.''

Nic's mouth thinned to a hard line. "There are a number of things you don't understand.''

"What things?''

"Things which have happened in my life during the last five years,'' Nic said starkly. "Events which are not pleasant even to recall . . .''

"I know . . . your wife's death,'' Cathy said a little less harshly, involuntarily moved by his obvious pain.

Nic turned to stare out of the window, his profile set like granite. "I am referring to Flavia's relationships with other men during the course of our marriage.''

Cathy stared at Nic aghast, wondering if she'd heard him properly.

"Y-your wife was unfaithful to you?'' It was hard to imagine any woman being married to Nic and being unfaithful to him.

Nic exhaled a sharp breath. "I assure you it's true.''

"I do . . . I mean, I don't disbelieve you . . . but why?'' Cathy murmured, still stunned by what Nic had said. He'd hinted that all hadn't been well in his marriage but when she'd seen his son yesterday, she'd assumed she'd been mistaken and that the union must have been a happy and secure one.

Nic swung back to face her. "The reasons do not matter. What matters is that perhaps you can now understand why I reacted as I did when I thought you had slept with me whilst engaged to another man.''

Cathy's heart seemed to turn over as she looked at him. Whatever had happened, how could she see him in pain . . . and he was in pain, she knew that now . . . and turn her back on him? How could she walk away from him now and not live with the regret of it forever?

She took a tentative step towards him, her hand reaching out to touch him. "Nic... I didn't realize."

Moments later his arms were folding round her possessively, drawing her against the hard length of his body. "Perhaps we should start again... no secrets this time."

She nodded, tears stinging the backs of her eyes. "Yes, let's start again."

His kiss was long and hard and very arousing. Then he glanced at his watch. "I promised Luc I'd take him to the coast for a picnic this afternoon. Want to come?"

She nodded happily. "Just give me a few minutes to change."

In the hour's drive from Florence, Nic had brought them to a long stretch of sandy beach near the small town of Alberese on the east coast. No buildings spoiled the rugged beauty of the area and the only concession to visitors were a few picnic tables and litter bins randomly situated among the tall pine trees which bordered the shore. It was an idyllic spot, deserted today, and perfect for a picnic.

To Cathy's relief, Luc had accepted her presence on the outing without question, bestowing on her the same gorgeous smile he had done yesterday and making her heart ache with the knowledge that such a little boy was having to grow up without a mother.

"Lei gioca a futbol?" Luc demanded in childish Italian, picking up the large football they'd brought with them.

Cathy laughed and explained with mock regret that she wasn't a very good footballer. *"Non sono una brava giocatrice."*

"But who can complain when there are so many other things you are good at?" Nic murmured meaningfully, his arm sliding round her waist and his gaze sliding appreciatively over her bikini-clad figure.

A faint blush stole over Cathy's cheeks. She'd slipped the bikini on hurriedly under her jeans and T-shirt back at the hotel. It was one she'd never worn before and she was a little surprised to discover that its subtle cut was deceptive, exposing a great deal more breast and thigh than she had expected it to.

"I love the way you blush like that," he laughed softly.

"Do you? Why?"

"You make me feel like the first man ever to arouse the woman in you."

"You were," she reminded him huskily.

His eyes darkened fractionally and his arm tightened on her waist. "Perhaps I should have said the *only* man."

That too, Cathy longed to tell him but wasn't sure if it was what he wanted to hear.

For almost two hours the three of them built sandcastles, collected shells, played football and paddled. Nic was exactly the sort of father Cathy had always thought he would be. Warm, affectionate, firm. There could be no doubt of how much he loved his son. It was there for anyone to see, in the way he ruffled Luc's hair, talked with him, explained things, made him chortle with laughter.

Once she had imagined what it would be like to bear Nic's children, and Cathy felt a horrible moment of heart-wrenching sadness as she acknowledged that Luc was Nic's son, conceived and borne by another woman.

When everyone had more or less run themselves ragged, they went back up the beach and settled down on one of the rugs for the picnic. If they had been dining in one of Italy's most stylish restaurants, she doubted they could have sat down to better fare.

They feasted on *bocconcini,* veal, ham and cheese mouthfuls, *sartu di riso,* a kind of rice pie with meat, mushrooms, tomatoes and cheese, *pizza rustica,* a farmhouse pizza, accompanied by *michette,* small round bread rolls and various salads and cheeses, followed by *bocconotti,* sweet pastries filled with aromatic jam, and *budino* mousse, together with apricots and peaches.

Nic had also brought a bottle of chilled Galestro wine, which he poured into two tall glasses and handed one to her.

"*Salute,*" he raised his glass to her, his eyes on hers.

"*Salute,*" Cathy murmured, almost unbearably conscious of his nearness.

"Now old was Luc when his mother died?"

There was a brief silence before Nic said, "Just under eighteen months old."

"He won't remember her," Cathy murmured, her heart melting as she gazed at the small boy tucking into his lunch. She'd been much older when her own father died, old enough to have known him at least. Luc wouldn't even have that.

"How do you manage? Looking after him, I mean?"

"He has a nanny. Antonietta . . . the woman you saw yesterday."

"Luc seems very fond of her," Cathy said, recalling how eagerly Luc had gone to her when she called him.

"He is. Unfortunately she's leaving soon. She is keen to travel and has got herself a job in America. I shall have to find a replacement."

"Will that be difficult?"

Nic's shrug was resigned. "I expect so. It usually is . . . to find the right one, that is."

Usually is! How many times had this happened? Cathy wondered. Luc couldn't be more than what...three and a half? How many nannies had he had since his mother died?

Luc had finished eating and had taken himself off to a rug beneath one of the trees and promptly fallen asleep, his darkly tanned limbs sprawled in chubby, childish innocence.

For a few moments, Cathy gazed at him, feeling her heart go out to him. He would be so easy to love...as easy as his father. The thought came to her like lightning and she swung her glance away. God! What was she thinking? She'd spent five years fighting *against* her love for this man.

She shifted her gaze and stared pensively out to sea, watching the rolling breakers sweep onto the smooth sweep of golden sand with rhythmic repetition.

"What are you thinking about?" Nic asked softly.

Cathy's mind floundered. Improvise—quickly, she demanded. "What I'm going to do when I go back to England. I've got to do some house hunting," she said, deliberately keeping her voice light.

"You're moving?"

She nodded. "Th-the flat I live in is going to be sold. It belongs to Graham, you see, and now that he and Cassie are getting married...well naturally, I'll have to move out...find somewhere of my own."

All at once she felt incredibly alone. Without warning, a tear trickled down her cheek and a sob trembled in her throat.

Suddenly Nic was beside her, his fingers closing on her chin, turning her face to his. The oddly sympathetic look she saw there only succeeded in making the tears run even faster down her cheeks.

"Don't, Cathy, don't. This man's not worth it...not if he's going to marry someone else."

He thought she was crying for Graham. He still thought she and Graham had been romantically involved. What a crazy, mixed-up mess this was.

She knew she should tell him the truth. There'd been too many misunderstandings between them already, but some instinct for self-preservation stilled her tongue.

"I'm not—"

"Like hell you're not," Nic derided.

Suddenly the mouth that covered hers wasn't gentle or sympathetic. It was hard and demanding.

She gasped as he pushed her back down onto the rug, his mouth going to her throat and then to an ear, taking the lobe and nipping it with his teeth.

"Did he make you feel like this?"

The thickly drawled question intruded on the breathless excitement building inside her. "Who?" she whispered dazedly.

"This man...this Graham."

Cathy shook her head. "No...never...only you," she murmured, incapable right now of denying the truth.

With a ragged groan of satisfaction, Nic's mouth came back to hers. "*Dios!* I want you...now...here," he groaned raggedly.

"I want you too," Cathy whispered shamelessly. "I always have."

Luc's yawning stretch took them both by surprise. Nic cast a glance at his slowly awakening son and then stretched out a hand to Cathy, pulling her upright to stand in front of him. His arm curved lightly round her waist.

"I suppose I should apologise for starting something here which was highly inappropriate given the public nature of our surroundings...and Luc's presence.'' Nic shot a swift glance in his son's direction. "That does not mean I regret it."

Cathy swayed against him, her body language as expressive as any words. Her fingers curved round his neck, drawing his mouth down to hers, lips softening beneath his.

"Dios!" Nic muttered roughly as his hold on her tightened. "If this is supposed to strengthen my will power, it's not going to work." He eased himself away from her, his fingers tracing the curve of her lips as if to take away the sting of separation. "Come back to Castel di Bellano with us for dinner."

Cathy swallowed and nodded. "Dinner would be fine." And supper...and breakfast, she thought breathlessly.

Seven

Nic's car had only just drawn up at the gravelled entrance to Castel di Bellano, when Antonietta came rushing down the steps to meet them, obviously very distressed. She cast an apologetic glance in Cathy's direction and then burst into a flood of Italian, so rapid that Cathy couldn't understand a single word.

The girl was almost crying as Nic gently ushered her back into the castle, speaking to her in low, urgent tones. Cathy took Luc's hand in hers and followed behind them.

"Nic, whatever's the matter?" she asked quickly as Antonietta darted off up the stairs.

"She's had a telephone call to say that her mother's been taken into hospital for emergency surgery. Her parents live in Potenza in southern Italy and naturally she wants to go down there straight away."

"Poor girl," Cathy murmured sympathetically.

"I'll drive her to the airport now. There's an internal flight within the hour."

"What can I do to help?"

Nic shook his head. "Quite honestly, the best thing you could do would be to stay here with Luc. Would you mind?"

"Of course I wouldn't," Cathy said, only too glad to be able to help in any way she could.

An hour later, she had given Luc his supper, bathed him and was sitting by the side of his bed, looking at a picture book with him. She could see his eyelids beginning to droop and knew he was getting sleepy. She snuggled him into the bed and then bent down to give him a kiss. His small arms curled round her neck as he kissed her back.

Downstairs again, she waited for Nic in the huge room where she had first met him. She felt more alive than she had done in years. In five years to be precise.

What if...? An idea occurred to her, one which she quickly dismissed. It was crazy. Or was it? Her lovely features frowned in contemplation of the possibilities.

At last she heard the crunch of Nic's car wheels on the gravel outside and minutes later the sound of a door slamming shut as he entered the house.

She hurried to greet him. "Did Antonietta get away alright?" He looked tired, she noted, and worried.

"Yes...eventually. Sorry I'm late. Her plane was delayed." Nic's arm slid round her waist, making her insides dissolve into delicious tremors. "I hope Luc behaved himself?"

"Of course he did..." Cathy paused, plucking up her courage. "In fact, I was going to ask how you're going to manage...looking after him, I mean... while Antonietta's away?"

"He's at nursery school in the mornings so that won't be a problem. As for the afternoons, I'll take some time off."

"Won't that be difficult at short notice?"

Nic shrugged. "These things happen."

Cathy took a deep breath and tried to keep her voice perfectly normal. "I've got a week's holiday coming up at the end of the week. I don't need to go back to England straight away. If you like, I could stay on and look after him...until Antonietta gets back, that is."

Nic stared at her for a moment, appearing to consider her suggestion, then said slowly, "I couldn't ask you to do that. It wouldn't be fair."

"You're not asking me, I'm offering," Cathy persisted, recklessly ignoring the warning bells which rang inside her head.

She was frightened of getting hurt again, frightened of getting too involved, but suddenly she knew she was just as frightened of losing Nic again.

Nic inhaled deeply. "Cathy...I don't want you to think I've misled you in any way. It's a generous offer and I'd be a fool if I didn't say it would help...or that I'd like to have you here..." His dark eyes flicked over her in a way which left no doubt of his meaning.

Somehow she managed to keep her voice casual. "Then it seems like a good arrangement for both of us. You get a temporary nanny and I get to spend a few more days in the Italian sunshine. The weather's been terrible in England recently."

"So," Nic demanded lazily, his expression mocking. "The weather is the main attraction, is it?"

"And Luc of course."

"No others?"

"What others could there possibly be?" she asked innocently.

Nic took a step towards her, drawing her into his arms, his victor's kiss quickly becoming deeper and more passionate, until both of them almost completely forgot where they were.

"Isn't this one of the reasons you want to stay?" Nic insisted huskily in her ear. "Because of the way I make you feel? Admit it?"

She stiffened slightly in his arms. "Because of the way *you* make *me* feel? Isn't it how I make you feel, too?"

"Of course it is, my sweet, Cathy," Nic soothed with honeyed words, his mouth moving to a trembling pulse in her throat. "That's what makes it so good. It's how we make each other feel...I want you as much as you want me. You know that."

There was both possession and tenderness in his eyes as he gazed down at her.

He couldn't look at her like that without caring just a little bit, could he?

How much more difficult was leaving going to be after sharing Nic's life—and bed—for a week? She frowned, pushing that disturbing thought aside. She'd worry about that when the time came. Not now.

"Mmm...what do you think?"

Cathy gazed at the painting's abstract design, angled her head and frowned. "What exactly is it supposed to *be*?"

Nic laughed. "Whatever you want it to be."

"But it must *be* something...I mean, I know I'm supposed to use my imagination and not just look for the literal but I really can't see anything in it beyond a few lines and squiggles."

"Well then, a few lines and squiggles is what it is."

Cathy shook her head. "There must be more to it than that?"

Nic slid her an amused look. "Why must there?"

Cathy was enjoying herself. She'd never been to an art exhibition before and she was fascinated by the range of paintings on display, some of which she liked enormously and some of which she considered infinitely inferior to those Luc brought home with him from nursery.

She'd been secretly pleased, too, at discovering that Nic had no reservations about bringing her with him to the invitation-only event for launching a number of new Italian artists. He obviously knew most of the other guests here but, even whilst mingling socially, he'd stayed by her side all evening, his arm occasionally circling her waist, making no attempt to disguise the fact that they were a couple.

Cathy's heart missed a beat. A couple, yes, but for how long? Antonietta had phoned earlier in the day to say that her mother was making a good recovery and should be well enough to leave alone within a day or two. What was going to happen then? She'd known from the beginning that it wouldn't be easy to leave but with each day which passed the prospect was becoming more and more unbearable.

She tried to brush away such bleak thoughts and forced her lips into some semblance of a smile to answer Nic's question. "Because it's not enough, I suppose. I can't see the point of painting something so... basic. It doesn't seem to have any purpose or meaning."

Nic swirled the ice cubes in his glass and then took a deep gulp of the contents. "Not everything has to be complicated to have purpose and meaning," he said evenly. "Don't you think something which is simple and straightforward can have its own value?"

Were they still just discussing paintings? Cathy wondered suddenly as an odd sensation shivered down her spine. Or was this as much about their different views on relationships as on art? "Surely there's a difference between some-

thing which is simple and something which is merely
superficial...? This painting seems to me to be superficial."

"Because it's so simple?"

"No...because there's no deeper meaning behind it."

Nic's dark eyes studied her. "Not everyone will be
searching for a deeper meaning. Some people will enjoy
looking at it just because it pleases them, nothing more."

"Maybe some people will."

"But not you?"

"No."

The denial earned her a narrow-eyed look from Nic.

All at once, Cathy knew she had been deceiving herself,
trying to convince herself that this time only her mind and
body were involved where Nic was concerned and that her
heart was safe. Of course her heart wasn't safe. She'd given
it to Nic five years ago and she'd never truly been able to
reclaim it.

You fool, she admonished herself bitterly. You love him,
you know you do. That's why you find the thought of losing
him again so terrifying.

Straightforward and uncomplicated, that's how Nic had
described the painting but that was how he wanted his relationships with women to be too, wasn't it?

Cathy and Nic went down to the swimming pool the fol-
lowing evening. Last night after the exhibition...and this
morning again...she'd intended to talk to him but somehow the moment had never seemed quite right. Now
though, she knew time was running out. Antonietta was due
back the next day. If she didn't do it soon, the opportunity
would be gone.

It was late, after nine o'clock. Luc was in bed, fast asleep, and the housekeeper had agreed to keep an ear open for him until they got back, since she still had some chores to finish.

The evening was warm and sultry and the water felt deliciously cool to Cathy as she executed a neat dive into the large oval pool. She struck out for the other end in a crawl and was soon conscious of Nic drawing alongside her, his strong arms cutting cleanly and easily through the water.

They completed several lengths side by side without stopping before pausing at one end.

"Mmm, I enjoyed that," Cathy murmured, pushing her wet hair back from her face.

"So did I," Nic agreed. "Though we could always make it a little more exciting." He grinned. "How about a race?"

Cathy shook her head and laughed. "I don't think so. You'd win easily."

"Not if I give you a head start."

"How big a start? Nine lengths over a ten-length distance?" she mocked. "Besides . . . what do I get out of it?"

"I'm sure I could think of a suitable incentive," Nic told her silkily, his eyes descending to her bikini-clad figure immersed beneath the water.

Heat pooled in the pit of Cathy's stomach as it always did when he looked at her like that. She deliberately tried to dampen it. She had to talk to Nic tonight about the future. Their future. She couldn't let that resolve simply dissolve into desire as it so often did as soon as he touched or even looked at her.

"Alright . . . you're on," she agreed quickly. "How about a two-length start?"

Almost before Nic could respond, she was pushing off, her arms rising and falling in regular strokes to cut cleanly through the water.

Cathy managed to remain ahead of Nic until the final length when he smoothly overtook her. She continued to the end but was out of breath when she finished, accepting Nic's extended hand gratefully and letting him pull her up onto the side to stand next to him.

"Can I claim my prize now?"

"What prize?"

"This." And he drew her against his slick, wet body, his mouth closing on hers, his tongue licking the moisture from her lips in slow, lazy strokes which sent darts of pleasure shooting the full length of her spine.

"Is there anything you don't do well?" she murmured huskily, when he finally released her.

His hard mouth curved in dry amusement. "I've reached an age where I've learned *only* to do what I do well."

"Well I haven't discovered any faults," Cathy insisted lovingly.

"That's only because you haven't been with me long enough."

The breath caught in Cathy's throat. She felt as if she was poised on the edge of a precipice. He'd given her the perfect opening. She just had to take her courage and leap in...

"Th-that could be remedied," she said shakily.

"What?"

She placed her hand on his chest, curling her fingers into the springy cloud of dark hairs which nestled there. "I don't have to go back to England. I could stay here ... with you."

"No!" His terse denial was so sharp that Cathy's hand fell from him as if she had been scalded.

Cathy shook her head, stunned by his reaction. "I thought you might *want* me to stay with you," she said jerkily.

An angry growl sounded deep in Nic's throat. "Let's not play games, Cathy. You want us to live together, don't you? That's what this is all about. Perhaps you're even thinking of marriage."

"And you don't want that?" Cathy said bleakly.

"No!"

Cathy had not thought it was possible to hurt so much. She could hardly believe that Nic could tell her that so brutally. Hot tears stung the backs of her eyes.

"You mean you don't want to see me any more once Antonietta returns?"

Nic's fingers bit painfully into her shoulders. "No, that is not what I mean. I come to England often and you can come to Italy. It is not the other side of the world. Of course we will still see each other."

What? Every few months? Every few weeks? A long distance affair? How could Nic possibly be satisfied with such an arrangement after the week they had just shared? How could she possibly bear it?

"But why, Nic? Why are you so adamant that we can't live together, at least? You care about me, I know you do."

Nic released her abruptly and half turned away, but she could still see the anguish in every hard-set feature.

"It is precisely because I care about you that I do not want us to live together. I've been married, Cathy. It didn't work."

"Perhaps because you were married to the wrong person," she said, desperation giving her the courage to continue. "Hasn't this last week shown you that?"

He gave a harsh laugh. "This last week was not marriage, Cathy. It was a honeymoon and like all honeymoons, ours would end."

"But why should that be so bad? Why can't it just be the beginning of something else? Something better?"

"Because it never is. I could only make you unhappy, *cara*, believe me. You would end up..." He stopped short.

Cathy reached out her fingers to touch the tense muscles of his shoulder. "You couldn't make me unhappy, Nic. Not being with you is going to make me unhappy, not the other way round. Won't you believe that?"

"Don't, Cathy, don't. It wouldn't work. I am no good at marriage, and it would not be fair to expect you to commit yourself to a relationship that may not last."

"I'm willing to take that chance."

"But I'm not."

His words were like daggers shooting into her heart. Feeling numb and icy inside, Cathy went across to where they'd flung their towelling robes on a chair, picked hers up and slung it round her shoulders.

Well, she'd talked to Nic. She'd taken her chance and lost. It was too late now for regrets.

They walked back to the house in silence and later, when they went to bed, it was the first time they did not make love.

Eight

Cathy had decided that she must at least stay on in Italy until Antonietta returned; to do anything else would be unfair to Luc.

Thus she collected Luc from nursery school as usual, arriving back at Castel di Bellano to find an unfamiliar car parked in front of the house. Just as they were approaching the front door, a woman opened it. A woman whom Cathy immediately recognised. La Signora Rossi. Cathy was surprised to see her but not nearly as surprised as when she saw Luc run to her in immediate recognition.

"Hello...Signora Rossi," Cathy greeted her a little uncertainly.

"*Buon giorno,*" the other woman returned calmly. "And please, call me Isabella. Now that you are no longer a guest at the hotel, there is no need for the formality of surnames."

Cathy was thoroughly mystified. It couldn't be Nic she'd come to see. She must know he was unlikely to be here at this time of day.

Isabella gave her a polite smile. "I was away this week on a course and did not know of Antonietta's absence or naturally I would have called earlier."

Naturally? Why naturally?

"I can see you are thinking that for someone who is only a member of Nicolas's staff, I am perhaps too closely involved with his family affairs," Isabella suggested coolly. "How could you possibly know that I am not only an employee of Nicolas but also a...a close friend."

A close friend? How close? Cathy wondered, feeling her throat tighten.

"I knew Nic long before he appointed me manageress of the Villa Annalisa."

"You did?"

Isabella nodded. "You see, Flavia—Nic's late wife—and I were best friends...almost sisters. Naturally, when she died, I did my best to comfort Nicolas in any way I could."

Cathy felt her pulse rate suddenly accelerate. This woman had been Flavia's best friend and what...Nic's lover? She inhaled a deep breath.

"You are here as Antonietta's temporary replacement, I understand."

Was it Nic who had described her as Antonietta's *temporary replacement?*

Somehow she got a grip on herself. "I offered to look after Luc as a favour, that is all."

Isabella eyed her up and down. "A favour that he much appreciated, I am sure."

Before Cathy could make any reply to that insinuative remark, Luc tugged on Isabella's hand, chattering away in a stream of Italian about his morning at the nursery.

Isabella listened attentively for a few minutes, then patted him on the head. *"Ho sete,"* she murmured, fanning herself with her hand. *"Ci porti per favore un succo di frutta."*

Obligingly Luc disappeared in the direction of the kitchen to ask for a cold drink for her.

"Shall we go and sit down on the terrace?" Isabella suggested.

Without any ready excuse to take herself off elsewhere, Cathy reluctantly moved in the direction of the patio terrace and sat down opposite Isabella at one of the wrought iron tables.

From a distance, it might have seemed as if they were two friends enjoying a casual chat. But close to, the tensions were obvious. Cathy could almost feel the hostile vibrations being emitted by the other woman. She knew now it was the same hostility she'd sensed on her first night in Florence, when the manageress had come to her bedroom and found Nic there. At least she understood it now. Isabella had obviously been involved with Nic in some way and as such resented any other woman's appearance in his life, however temporary.

"You knew Nicolas several years ago, before his marriage, I understand," Isabella said abruptly.

"That's right," Cathy agreed briefly, her pulse quickening a little.

"You will have seen some changes in him, I am sure. He has been a different man since Flavia died so tragically."

"H-how did Flavia die?" she heard herself asking.

Isabella frowned, her expression betraying surprise and not a little satisfaction. "You do not know? I assumed Nicolas would have told you."

Cathy shook her head.

A look of genuine pain darkened Isabella's face. "A car accident. On the road to Castel di Bellano."

Cathy paled. "How terrible," she murmured.

"Yes, it was terrible," Isabella agreed, her eyes narrowing. "Especially since there was not one life lost but two."

"The driver of the other car, you mean?"

The question hung in the air for several seconds before Isabella answered slowly. "No. Flavia was pregnant."

Cathy's lungs seemed to be hurting and it was an effort even to breathe. "Pregnant?" she repeated numbly. "But I thought that Nic and...and Flavia had some...some problems in their marriage."

Isabella made a dismissive sound deep in her throat. "They were both young and self-willed, naturally they had fights now and then. Italian marriages are like that. But they loved each other very much. Flavia would not have been pregnant if there had not been as much loving as fighting, would she?"

Of course she wouldn't, Cathy acknowledged bleakly. Was this fiery, volatile, passionate relationship the reality? Not the estranged, unhappy one she had envisaged?

Estranged! How estranged could a couple be if the wife was pregnant? Oh God! She'd been killed when she was carrying his child. No wonder Nic was so bitter.

"Nic blamed himself," Isabella said tautly. "He had been abroad for several days on business and Flavia was hurrying to get home to see him. It was not his fault, of course, but he has always felt partly responsible."

Cathy felt as if a knife was being twisted inside her. No wonder Nic couldn't contemplate another serious relationship when he was still carrying all that grief and guilt from his marriage. Why hadn't he told her?

She struggled to focus her thoughts back on Isabella.

Isabella shrugged. "It is fortunate, at least, that Nicolas and I have been able to console each other. We have found great solace in each other's company during the last two years.''

There could be no doubt of Isabella's meaning. She was telling Cathy very plainly that her relationship with Nic had not merely been the platonic one of a friend helping out at a time of grief. She'd been his lover and she wanted him for herself.

And wasn't that truly what Nic wanted too? A lover who was willing to accept his refusal to commit himself to a deeper relationship, a woman who accepted that he'd loved his wife deeply and would never fully get over her loss, someone who accepted that, for him, she would always be second best.

A simple, uncomplicated relationship, with no deeper meaning, just like the painting.

Before Cathy could say anything, Luc appeared round the corner, accompanied by the housekeeper, who was carrying a tray laden with a jug of fruit juice and a couple of tall glasses.

Evidently though, Isabella wasn't as thirsty as she had thought. She got up swiftly and glanced at her watch. "I'm afraid I must be going," she said, turning to Cathy and adding pointedly. "I expect this is goodbye. I doubt we'll meet again before you leave."

Somehow Cathy doubted it too.

Cathy gazed down from the aeroplane window as Florence faded from sight below her and she continued to gaze down long after cloud cover had obscured the city from sight.

Nic was down there . . . somewhere. Soon he would be returning to Castel di Bellano and then he would find her note. How would he react? Would he be glad that it had finished like this? Would he be relieved to be spared more embarrassing declarations of love and need from her?

Cathy closed her eyes, trying to force back the hot tears which pressed against her lids.

Where had she found the strength to get through the last few hours? Once Isabella had left, she had continued to sit numbly at the table, watching Luc play with his trucks and buckets in the sand pit.

Whether Isabella and Nic had been lovers hardly seemed to matter. She didn't blame or condemn Nic for seeking comfort where he could after Flavia's death. What hurt so badly was the knowledge that he had lied to her, implicitly if not explicitly. He had let her believe that his marriage to Flavia had been unhappy. He had certainly never told her that Flavia had been expecting his child when she died.

But, of course, once she knew the truth, so many questions were answered. She knew why Nic didn't want to make their relationship permanent. Just as she knew why he couldn't love her.

It was Luc's noisy greeting which had jerked her from her reverie and alerted her to the fact that a car had drawn up at the house. At first she'd been terrified that it was Nic but in fact it was Antonietta, smiling and holding out her arms to welcome Luc into them.

She looked much more relaxed than she had done when Cathy had last seen her and she smiled happily when Cathy enquired about her mother.

"She is much better. Quite well now. Thank you. And how is Luc? Has he been a good boy?"

Cathy tried to ignore the numbness creeping round her heart as she assured Antonietta that he had been very, very good. She could barely bring herself to look at Luc.

"In fact, I'll be sad to leave him." The slight tremor in her voice betrayed just how sad.

Antonietta gave her a questioning look. "You are leaving?"

Cathy nodded vigorously, her nails pressing tightly into the palms of her hands. "Yes...straight away, in fact, now that you are back. I won't have any difficulty getting on a flight to England if I leave at once."

"But I thought Mr. Lucciano said—"

"There's a problem at my office in England," Cathy interrupted hurriedly. "Mr. Lucciano doesn't know. I'll leave him a note and explain."

Cathy felt terrible as she saw the other girl's confused and concerned look.

"Should you not wait and speak to him?"

"No!" Cathy's stomach felt as if it was twisting itself into knots. "No...he'll understand," she said, trying to keep the mounting tension from her voice. "Once he reads my note, he'll understand."

Would he understand? she wondered now as she leaned her head back into her aeroplane seat and closed her eyes. Of course he would. He would understand and agree that it was better things should end like this rather than dragging on over weeks or months.

Nine

"My God! Honey, you look dreadful," Sally told her bluntly the next morning. "What the hell's the matter with you? When I told you to sample the Italian men, wine and food, I meant one at a time not have an orgy."

Cathy attempted a weak smile. "Very funny. I...er...just didn't sleep very well last night, that's all."

"Feeling lonely were you?"

Cathy's eyes lost their dull glaze for a moment. How did Sally know? In fact, her bed had felt lonely. She'd tossed and turned restlessly, her arms reaching out in the empty space beside her for a hard, male body, but it hadn't been there. And each time she'd woken, the loneliness had seemed even more unbearable.

"Why should I have been feeling lonely?" she demanded cagily.

Sally gave her a sly smile. "Honey, I may be approaching middle age but I'm not losing my marbles. You've got man trouble written all over you. I'm right, aren't I?"

"Yes, alright, you're right," Cathy told her grittily, too exhausted and dispirited to deny it. "There *was* a man. *Was*, note. There isn't any longer, so can we please just leave it there?'' She really didn't feel up to coping with her out-spoken, American editor right now.

Sally gave her a narrow-eyed look and said more gently, ''You've got it pretty bad, haven't you?''

''What?''

''Love, honey. It's written all over you.''

''Don't worry, it'll fade soon,'' Cathy said bleakly.

''What's up, kid? He obviously did something pretty bad. He didn't dump you for another woman did he?''

If it hadn't been so heart-wrenchingly painful, Cathy might have been tempted to laugh. In a way, Sally was right. She had been dumped—for a ghost!

''No, he didn't,'' she said firmly, knowing that to agree would only open up a contorted maze of explanations which she wasn't up to right now.

''Then why—?''

''Sally, please, could we just drop this? I really don't want to talk about it. Now, about those reviews...''

An hour later found Cathy gazing bleakly out of the window, her thoughts miles away. How she'd hated leaving Luc. The poor child had had so many losses in his life already and her going had made it yet one more.

She'd tried her best to explain in stilted Italian that she had to get back to England, but how could a three-year-old possibly understand? She missed him, missed the feel of his warm, little body in her arms as much as she missed his father. It was almost unbearable to know that she would never see either of them again.

The intercom buzzing loudly on her desk almost made her jump out of her shoes.

''Yes?''

''Cathy, I've got someone here to see you... Sorry, sir, what did you say your name was again?''

There was a muffled noise in the background and then Cathy heard the receptionist's agitated voice insist, "I'm sorry, sir... you can't go through there... not until..." Then, apologetically, "Cathy, I'm terribly sorry. He's just disappeared down the corridor. I think he must be coming to find you. Do you want me to call Security?"

The tall dark figure appearing in the doorway caused Cathy's head to lift in his direction. Nic! What on earth was he doing here?

"Cathy... are you alright... do you want me to call Security?" the receptionist asked urgently.

Cathy's throat felt so tight that it was a struggle to say anything. "No... it's okay," she managed at last. "I'm quite safe."

"Do not be so damn sure," Nic imparted grimly as he stared at her across the room. "The way I feel right now is positively murderous. What the hell did you think you were doing, running away from me like that?"

"I did not run away," Cathy retorted, piqued by his accusing tone. "I left you a note."

"A note to tell me you were running away."

"A note to explain why I was leaving," she corrected tautly, standing up to face him.

"It makes no difference," Nic dismissed with an arrogant tilt of his shoulders. "You ran away."

"What does it matter?" Cathy demanded impatiently. "Don't pretend to be sorry that I left."

Nic took a step towards her, his eyes almost black. "If you think I am pretending to be sorry, then you are badly mistaken..."

Cathy's heart plummeted to her feet. He wasn't even sorry she'd gone. He'd just admitted as much.

His eyes narrowed. "I am not sorry. I am bloody furious with you for what you did."

His expression did indeed look almost murderous, and for the first time Cathy felt a frisson of fear assault her senses. "Nic... this is hardly the place for this discussion."

"No, it certainly isn't," Sally agreed, striding into the office with all the authority her petite frame would permit. "Oh!" She stopped dead when she saw Nic and eyed him up and down, her gaze sliding appreciatively over his tall frame. "Who are you?"

"Nicolas Lucciano," Nic returned grimly. "Who are you?"

"I'm Sally Jackson. Cathy's editor." Those words seemed to remind Sally that she was here to do more than simply ogle the man standing in front of her and she said, a little more authoritatively, "I'm afraid I'm going to have to ask you to leave. We simply can't have strange men—"

"I'm not a stranger, I'm a friend of Cathy's," Nic interrupted her.

"Is this true?" Sally demanded, turning to Cathy.

"No it's not," Cathy retorted angrily. Friends didn't lie to each other and deceive each other! Not in her book!

Nic's smouldering gaze settled on her. "Alright then," he agreed silkily. "I'm not her friend, I'm her lover..."

He ignored Cathy's shocked intake of breath to continue, "...and I'm shortly going to be her husband."

Cathy gripped the edge of her desk tightly. The events of the last twenty-four hours had somehow distorted her sense of reality. Nic wasn't really here at all and he certainly wasn't proposing marriage. She closed her eyes, certain that when she opened them again, the world would be set right once more but amazingly nothing looked any different. Nic was still glaring at her across the room and Sally, for once, was utterly speechless.

"Is this true?" Sally squeaked when she finally got some movement back in her vocal cords.

"No, of course it isn't," Cathy denied hotly.

"Of course it is," Nic corrected smoothly, bestowing a devastatingly sexy smile on Sally. "So, you see, Cathy's in very safe hands."

Sally seemed to turn to limpid jelly before Cathy's very eyes. She smiled back at Nic. "You've convinced me," she told him throatily, heading for the door.

"Sally, wait a minute, you can't just leave me—"

"Honey, I think this is one time when you don't need a chaperone. The man's going to marry you."

"No he isn't."

Sally winked at Nic. "If you can't convince her, come and knock on my door instead. I assure you I won't be nearly so difficult to persuade." And with that, she went out, shutting the door firmly behind her.

Cathy's mouth curved belligerently. "Do you mind telling me what all that was about? You have no intention of marrying me."

Nic started to move towards her. "Correction, I *had* no intention of marrying you. I've changed my mind, that's all."

Cathy jabbed a pencil furiously in the air. "So? I'm supposed to gratefully accept, am I? Well, I've changed my mind too. I don't want any kind of long-term relationship with you and I'm certainly not going to marry you."

Nic was on the other side of her desk now, his body so close that she could feel its familiar pull on her senses. But he didn't make any attempt to touch her. He simply said, "Cathy, will you let me explain?"

"Isabella *explained* everything."

"No, she didn't. She couldn't. She doesn't know everything."

"She knows she wants you," Cathy said bitterly.

"Maybe so," Nic agreed without a shred of arrogance. "But she can't have me. I'm yours. I always have been."

"Always? Don't lie, Nic. You married Flavia because you loved her and you still love her."

Nic shook his head. "You're wrong on every count, Cathy. I never loved Flavia, that was the trouble." Then, at Cathy's frowning look, "There's a lot of things I haven't told you. I met Flavia just over four years ago...in a nightclub...when she was working in Florence for the summer."

Cathy didn't know whether she really wanted to hear about the hectic social life Nic had been enjoying four years before whilst she was breaking her heart over him in England.

"I won't go into all the details but pretty soon we were involved in an affair."

Cathy's body stiffened and she tried to turn away but Nic's fingers tightened on her shoulders. "Listen, Cathy, please. We must talk about this. If it's any consolation," he added bitterly, "I don't much like the story either."

"It wasn't long before Flavia told me she was pregnant. I hadn't planned for that. You see, I didn't love her. I'd made that very clear to her early on in our relationship. Quite frankly, and you may not like hearing this either, all I wanted was an affair. As far as I was concerned, we were two unattached adults who enjoyed each other's company."

"That's obviously not all it was to Flavia," Cathy interrupted, feeling an unexpected wave of sympathy for the unknown Flavia. "She must have loved *you,* even if you didn't love her."

"Will you let me finish," Nic sighed. "Flavia had told me she was on the pill, that there was no danger of her getting pregnant. Afterwards she admitted it had been a lie. From the beginning, she'd decided to get pregnant, knowing that I would feel compelled to marry her, and she was right."

It was the oldest trick in the book, Cathy thought, her initial sympathy for Flavia dissolving a little.

"I never lied to Flavia," Nic resumed rawly. "She knew I didn't love her, but equally she knew I would do what I could to make our marriage work."

"And did it?"

A grim look penetrated Nic's eyes. "I wanted it to work, especially after Luc was born. Given that I'd married Flavia without loving her, I suppose I never really expected to love Luc, either. Oh, I know that sounds a terrible thing to say but I didn't. No one was more amazed than I at how I felt when I first held him in my arms."

"Surely the love you *both* felt for Luc must have helped?"

"You'd think so, wouldn't you, but you'd be wrong. You see, Flavia hated motherhood. She soon grew tired of looking after Luc and found him a burden. The fact that she knew how much I loved him seemed to make it worse. It was as if she came to blame Luc for taking the love which she felt rightly belonged to her. Soon she was spending hardly any time at home. Luc rarely even saw her."

"Oh, Nic! It must have been terrible," Cathy murmured.

"It was," Nic agreed. "But it got worse. Flavia started to have affairs. I think she hoped that if she could make me jealous and angry enough that it would make me love her. Of course, it only created more furious arguments. Gradually we became more and more estranged. Flavia took to going off for days at a time with other men."

"But, Nic. She was pregnant when she died. Isabella told me so. She was hurrying home to greet you."

Nic nodded grimly. "She was pregnant, yes, but not with my child. We hadn't slept together the last year of her life."

Cathy tried to stifle her startled gasp.

"And she wasn't coming *to* Castel di Bellano, she was leaving it. She told me that she'd found someone else, a wealthy, middle-aged American who was besotted with her and, what was worse, she was taking Luc with her. That's why I followed her that day, to try to get Luc back. I knew our marriage was over but I couldn't let her take Luc. She didn't love him. When her car crashed and she was killed, I was consumed with guilt. I thought that if I hadn't been chasing after her the accident might never have happened."

"But it wasn't your fault," Cathy told him, her fingers gently caressing his hard-set jaw. "You didn't have any choice but to do what you did...for Luc's sake."

"Maybe not but I still felt responsible. That was why, when the inquest revealed that Flavia had been pregnant, I let everyone believe that the child had been mine. Flavia's life had been so short and so tragic that there seemed no point in blackening her name after her death with details of her infidelity. It was the only thing left I could do for her."

Cathy's heart melted as she considered what Nic had tried to do for Flavia. Another man would have welcomed the opportunity to blacken his wife's name after such treatment, but Nic hadn't.

"But didn't Isabella know all this?" she asked softly.

Nic shook his head. "No. Of course she knew we'd had some problems in our marriage, but I don't think she ever knew just how bad things were. For some reason, Flavia never told her the whole truth. Pride partly, I think. Flavia always admired Isabella. I don't think she wanted her to know that her marriage was a failure. Afterwards, there seemed no point in destroying Isabella's illusions with the cold, harsh facts. What good would it have done?"

Cathy thought back to what Isabella had said. But what about her insinuation that she and Nic had had an affair?

"She suggested that you and she had had an affair." Cathy told him quietly.

"We didn't," Nic denied brusquely. "An affair between us was never on the cards. I liked and admired Isabella but I never wanted our relationship to be intimate. She lost Flavia and her job in Milan within months of each other. That was why I bought the Villa Annalisa and installed her as manageress. I hoped it would give her life some purpose. If she suggested that there was more to our relationship than friendship, then she was lying, Cathy. There's been no other woman in my life but Flavia and even then, I didn't love her. How could I? I loved you."

Tears dampened Cathy's cheeks. "I want to believe you, Nic. But how can I when only two days ago, you told me you didn't want us to even live together, let alone marry? How can I believe that you can love me?"

Nic's fingers brushed the tears away. "Cathy, *cara,* don't cry. I know now that I fell in love with you five years ago and I've never stopped loving you in all that time. After you left Florence, my pride was so badly hurt by what I thought you'd done that I didn't want it to be true that I loved you. But it was. That's why I could never love Flavia . . . because

I was already in love with you. Only I wouldn't accept the truth of that until I got back to Castel di Bellano yesterday and found your note. I was furious with you for leaving me. I got the first available plane to England, determined to tell you just how angry you had made me. And on the journey, I had to ask myself why I was so angry.

"You see, after Flavia died I convinced myself that I wasn't capable of loving anyone, that I would only bring unhappiness and pain to any other woman I got too deeply involved with. But it isn't true. I couldn't love Flavia because I already loved you. Yesterday, when I realized how empty my life would be without you in it, I saw the truth at last. It's you I love, Cathy. I always have done. I know I can make you happy... I know we can make each other happy. You will marry me, won't you?"

Cathy stared at him, hardly able to believe that any of this could really be true. It felt too much like a fairy story.

Her eyes searched his face and saw the love and need there, which mirrored her own. "Oh, Nic, darling. Of course I will," she agreed huskily. "I've never stopped loving you, either. You know there's been no other men in my life in all those years. It wasn't just that Graham wasn't my lover, there was no one else, either. I knew I could never settle for second best."

A loud "Mmmm" in the doorway interrupted the long, passionate kiss which followed that admission.

"Is this a private orgy or can anyone join in?" Sally enquired dryly. "Do I take it you two have decided on a merger and agreed to terms and conditions?"

Cathy nodded happily. "I'm afraid the bride's position is filled... but there is still an opening for a bridesmaid."

Sally's eyes lit up. "You know, I've never been a bridesmaid before and I've always fancied myself in pink organza..."

Cathy's mouth curved in a smile. "Something tells me I'm going to regret this."

"No, you're not," Nic whispered as his arm slid round her waist and drew her close against him. "I promise there will be no regrets. No regrets at all."